# Death Cult

Janelle Schiecke

Emerald Link Press

Book Cover by Ben Mcleod

To my loving husband—who has always supported my creative journey—and to my brilliant son, whose mind is a trove of wonder and intrigue.
Much love to my two wonderful brothers, and thank you for your support.

Everybody is a book of blood; wherever we're opened, we're red.

Clive Barker

# Contents

## Prologue

Sweat dripped from his pores, and his chest heaved with each ragged breath. If he were able to see the upside-down cross painted on his face in fresh blood, he'd notice the outline was washing away. The vertical line running from the bottom of his chin to the middle of his forehead had fleshy streaks where the sweat had trickled down, and the horizontal line running from both cheeks along his mouth was jagged at best. The matte of long, black hair that clung to his clammy flesh was somehow suffocating. He knew it would come to this; he just didn't know it would be so soon. But dark promises run deep.

The room was dimly lit by the ring of flickering candles placed on the cold concrete below him. He knew what this room looked like... yards of concrete stretching out around him, the center stained a deep red. And the smell, oh the smell... That pungent, metallic scent was the rank of countless others who had perished before him. He'd been in here before to witness the bloodshed. And now, it would be his sacrifice. His throat was on fire, cut from his jagged screams. It couldn't be his time yet, surely there was still more to do for his brethren and his master. But fate was not his to control, and it never was. None of them knew when they would surrender their flesh.

The circular steel contraption his naked body was splayed on reached above his head. The thin vertical pole was cold against his back, and his arms and legs were pulled taut to the edges of the circle. Wriggling his wrists, he felt the thick steel clamps dig into his skin and winced at the pain. Beautiful, necessary pain. The thick clamps around his ankles dug to the bone. As he saw his brethren slowly filter in, their heads bowed down, he briefly closed his eyes. The time was near. Though his heart still pounded from within, his breathing slowed to a steady rhythm. In and out... birth to death.

They began their low chant, the chant he had uttered so many times before. Somehow it danced from their lips now, almost dreamlike. Then, with one loud beat of a hand drum, it stopped. Silence fell... until the giant circular blade located directly beneath him and between his legs began to whir—slow at first, the rotations almost countable. Then it erupted into a fury, the sharp sound of steel teeth cutting through the air.

His chest puffed out with each inhale, eyes wide and panicked. The leather strap beneath his chin prevented him from looking down, and all he could do was wait. As the large metal saw spun and taunted, its slow ascent dragged out the inevitable. But he knew... he knew when those first few blades would cut through his skin. And when they finally did, the insurmountable pain seared through him like wildfire. He tried to scream, but the leather strap under his jaw held his mouth shut. Nostrils flaring, his eyes rolled in their sockets. He could feel his flesh being torn open one layer at a time, and was on the verge of passing out. Just as the metal teeth reached his intestines, everything went black.

Steamy entrails splattered to the concrete floor as the saw relentlessly spun upward, cutting his body completely in half.

# 1

## Road Trip

The desolate Nevada landscape stretched out before them, an endless arid desert of sagebrush and cacti. Jason's red Fox Body Mustang had a quarter tank left, and he worried they wouldn't make it to the next gas station. A thirsty V-8 sat under the hood. As he drove on, he eyed Eddie in the passenger seat, who was now fast asleep. Eddie's elbow rested on the passenger door, the back of his hand against the glass and his cheek smashed against his palm. His head bobbed with each bump in the pavement, and drool was beginning to drip from the corner of his mouth. Jason didn't know what drugs his friend was on last night, but judging from his deep sleep, it had to be something good.

Jason had only known Eddie for three weeks now—three weeks of almost nonstop partying, drinking, and sex. He wished he'd gotten the number of the girl he slept with last night under the speckled Nevada sky. Her blue eyes glistened in the moonlight and her soft blonde hair brushed against his chest as she rode him. And her breasts... those wonderful breasts. So soft, so supple, so—

"Where the fuck *are* we?" Eddie's voice jarred Jason's sensual reverie.

Looking at him, Jason pursed his lips in disappointment. "Hell if I know. Shit, I'm just trying to get back to the highway, but... I think we're lost, man. Took a wrong turn." He was worried, but he knew it would work out. It *always* worked out. Soon enough, there would be a sign for I-80.

Eddie grimaced slightly, then asked, "You score last night?"

"Yeah, I did. You?"

"*Fuck* yeah! All weekend, baby!"

Jason rolled his eyes. "Lucky you." He'd never been the promiscuous type. Hell, he was still pining over the only girl he slept with all weekend—those soft, gentle curves still playing in his memory.

"So, we're not headed out east?"

"We'll get there. Just... Can you grab the map out of the center console? I *swear* this road leads to I-80."

Eddie clumsily opened the center console like it was the hardest thing to do, grunting with each excessive effort. Finally, he procured the large paper map and began wrestling with it like it was an alligator. Jason marveled at Eddie's carelessness and pulled over. "We need a break. I feel like I've been driving in circles. Let's figure this shit out."

Still fumbling with the map, Eddie asked, "How does anyone *read* these things?"

"You didn't... Oh yeah, I forgot—you hitchhiked here."

"These beauties do me good." Eddie held up his thumbs and bent them back, classic hitchhiker style. He did have perfect thumbs for the job, Jason couldn't deny it. Bent at the knuckles like champs.

Once Jason parked the car, Eddie stepped out and stretched his arms above him. Grabbing the map, Jason walked to the front of his car and sat on the hood. He surmised their surroundings while looking at the unfolded paper before him riddled with a sea of meandering lines and symbols. It seemed they were in the middle of nowhere—he couldn't even pinpoint their location. Desolate pavement stretched out before them, disappearing under a blazing sun that was beginning its slow descent. They had to figure this out before nightfall. He shuddered at the thought of being stranded in his hatchback at the mercy of the sprawling Nevada desert.

Jason had met Eddie at a drug-fueled party that ended their college graduation with a bang. Turned out he'd hooked up with a girl that night whose best friend had hooked up with Eddie. When he discovered Eddie craved a summer escape just like he did, they'd pretty much been inseparable. So, to celebrate the beginning of a cross-country road trip, away from all the shit that would be waiting for them when they got back, they attended a rock music festival near Red Rock Canyon last night. The sparkling vast canopy against fathomless gray still hung in his mind. Desert skies at night were a sight to be seen.

Jason dug Eddie's carefree vibe, and he supposed Eddie enjoyed his esoteric ways. They both had that in common—an open mind and an appreciation for the hidden corners of life overlooked by most. And now, here they were, escaping the doldrums of everyday life in search of a good time. The summer of '84 was gonna be killer. Fuck college exams, and fuck goddamn schedules. Jason had other reasons for escaping, too. His mom's death still clung to him, and he desperately sought to numb the pain. As for Eddie, partying and adventure just ran in his blood.

After running his fingers in rumination through his black, feathered hair, Jason pinched his chin. He glanced at Eddie, who had taken off his shirt and was soaking in the last of the sun's muted rays before it slept below the horizon. Smoke wafted through the air from the cigarette now held in Eddie's fingertips, and his plaid flannel was tied around his waist. Not a bad choice... The heat was still sweltering and he felt the sweat drip from every part of his body. Eddie was muscular and trim from all the rock climbing he did, while Jason was just... scrawny. For all the late-night pizza he ate while gaming, he had to thank a high metabolism for fighting the bulge. But despite their physical differences, they were one and the same. Two dudes who had just quit low-level jobs to enjoy an epic summer on the road. California girls were hot, but Midwest girls? They were a whole different breed, baby.

"Why don't we just find somewhere to stay the night? Head out first thing in the morning?" Eddie was stretching as he spoke, and noticed Jason's confused expression. "Yoga. Never heard of it? Yeah, it's new. Supposed to keep you all flexible and shit. Helps me out, tell you that. Especially with the *ladies*."

"To each their own, man. I wouldn't be caught dead doin' that shit. But you're right. If we can find somewhere, that'd be good. Talk to someone, get directions to the freeway." He folded the map back up, placed it into his right hand, and tapped it lightly on his left palm. The sun wasn't skipping a beat, and it had begun to resemble a blood orange. "We're bound to run into something. C'mon, let's go." They both stepped back into the car, Jason opting to drive again. Being naturally complacent, Eddie was fine with that.

The road continued on forever with no sign of life, and they were both beginning to fret. But just as Eddie raised his hand to voice his concern, they saw a motel sign on the horizon.

"Holy! Ah, shit! *Finally*, man!" Eddie slapped one of his knees in fervid excitement.

"About fucking t—" There was a loud thump, and Jason slammed the brakes. He looked at Eddie, who wore the same expression—the one someone sports when they realize they just ran a large animal over. "Uh... What was *that?*" Jason looked through the rearview mirror to find a small mass lying on the pavement behind them, but he couldn't quite make it out.

"Welp, only one way to find out." Eddie opened his door, and Jason followed suit. The sun had just dipped below the mountains, illuminating the landscape in a dreamy orange hue. As they walked slowly to what lay on the pavement, Eddie's eyes grew wide and he covered his gaping mouth with his hand. That nebulous hue had suddenly turned nightmarish.

Jason squinted his eyes, incredulous. "Is that... is that what I *think* it is?"

"Sure is." Eddie placed his hands on his hips and shook his head, appalled. "Holy *fuck!*"

Lying before them on the gritty pavement was a human arm. Looked like it had been ripped clean from the socket, and the meat was mostly eaten down to the bone. Maggots squirmed in and out of the tissue, and Jason fought the urge to vomit. He stepped back, shaking his head and looking wide-eyed at Eddie. "Dude, where the fuck *are* we?"

# 2

## Dark Tomb

Carrie had sprained her ankle in the fall, but thankfully nothing felt on the verge of being broken or fractured. Shattered sticks covered the floor surrounding her—she'd heard them crack when the thin layer gave. Looking up at the opening above her, she raised her hand to her brow to block the blinding afternoon sunlight. A bright blue sky looked down on her from above, wistful cotton ball clouds floating by. They continued their slow trek as she lay here, here... where the hell *was* here? She'd fallen probably ten feet into a concrete room with two rectangle openings resembling doorways, yet there were no doors. One opening stood to her right, and the other one behind her.

Feeling incredulous about her current situation, she placed her palms firmly on the ground and craned her neck to assess her surroundings in more detail. Suddenly, the faint sound of footsteps resonated from the opening behind her. Turning at her waist to peer into it, all Carrie saw was fathomless black. The footsteps continued to scurry along, slowly becoming louder now. Their erratic footfall triggered the sixth sense in her stomach to light up... *danger*. Standing up and wincing at the pain in her ankle, she limped toward the opposite opening. Peering in, she noticed it led to an ascending concrete stairwell. Knowing she didn't stand a chance at escaping above, she took her chances and limped up the stairwell.

Cringing with each painful step, she finally arrived at the top. Behind her now was a stone wall, and a long hallway ran in front of her. It led to a room containing what looked like some kind of metal device—a large circular structure with a pole running up the middle. Flickering candles had been placed in a circle on the ground surrounding it. Walls ran along each side of the hallway with arched openings along them, about waist height. The openings were just large enough for her body to fit into, and as she heard the footsteps ascending the stairwell behind her, she pressed her luck again and climbed into the first open arch. As she did so, her sneakers touched something hard and knobby. It made a clank on the concrete and she scuffed it away, in turn hitting something else that made a slightly louder sound.

She reached her right arm to her left shoulder to slide the backpack off, wanting to grab her flashlight.

But the footsteps resonated on the other side of the wall now, so she carefully knelt down, hiding from the opening of the archway and stepping slightly to the left. Covering her mouth with her hand so she wouldn't make a sound, Carrie concentrated on taking slow, deep breaths. Tears blurred her vision, and she blinked her eyes to clear them. The footsteps continued down the hallway, then stopped. A head poked through one of the archways further down and she stifled a scream, remaining as still as a statue. Then she heard a grunt resonate from the direction of the large room, and the head disappeared.

Several other garbled voices joined in, and though she tried to discern what they were saying, she couldn't make out any words. It just sounded like utterances. After waiting for what felt like an eternity, the voices and footsteps finally subsided as they traveled away. Taking a deep breath in, she then closed her eyes and sighed out in relief. *That was a close one.* Feeling safe now to remove her backpack from her shoulders, she slowly did so, every small movement taking minutes. The scant light from the candles filtering in wasn't much, and she was practically surrounded by darkness. Rummaging through her backpack, her fingers found her small flashlight. *Thank God.* She'd packed it when she went spelunking a few weeks ago with friends, and had fortuitously not removed it. If the flashlight was in there, then her static line probably was, too. Rummaging through some more, she closed her eyes in overwhelming relief as her fingertips touched the rough rope. She'd surely find a use for that as well.

Removing the flashlight from her bag, Carrie took a deep breath in, steeling herself for what she would discover lurking in the thick darkness with her. When she clicked the power button on and shined the light before her, a mound of human bones was visible. Dropping the flashlight, she tried to scuttle back, realizing there was nowhere to go. The concrete wall at the end of the confine was hard against her back. Eyes widening with horror, she breathed in small, quick breaths. Her heart hammered against her chest and fear flooded her body, instantly tightening every muscle.

In a feeble motion, she picked up the flashlight and shined it to her left and to her right, noticing she was in quite a tight space. The length of the confine ran the length of the hallway, but it was only about four feet wide. Every surface from floor to ceiling was concrete, and the floor was practically covered in human bones. *Oh, Carrie. What have you done?*

A man's scream erupted from down the hallway now—loud and anguished. The screaming continued until his voice became weak and raspy. And still, it cut through his throat into the darkness, echoing within the concrete tomb. His bloodcurdling screams were accompanied by footsteps again and humming. No... *chanting*. She couldn't make out what they were saying. It was that same incoherent sound—low and guttural. As the voices became closer, she clicked off her flashlight and sat still with her back against the concrete wall. Closing her eyes, she continued to sob as her shoulders heaved. The man's anguish was so palpable, and his pain seemed to seep into her very being.

After a short time, the footsteps stopped and she heard the sound of metal clanging. Was he being attached to the metal device? The screams eventually subsided, but the chanting continued. It began as melancholy in nature, then erupted into baneful wails. The jagged edges of their chaotic invocation pierced through her very brain, and she cringed under their wrath. When the haunting chorus at last came to an end, dead silence followed. Carrie's eyes darted in every direction, anticipating a hand launching through one of the arched openings, but instead she heard the sound of a saw. *Oh my God!* As the saw picked up pace and whirred into a violent frenzy, she closed her eyes and covered her ears with her hands. This did little to dampen the horrifying shriek of metal, and she knew what was going to come next.

There was a wet sound as the blades came in contact with flesh, and then incessant dull whirs as it cut through bone. All she could do was cower and cry as the man in the room down the hallway was sawed to death.

# 3

## UNSETTLING WELCOME

After they'd run over a goddamn *human arm*, Jason especially wanted to hightail it out of there. He and Eddie both knew their chances of finding another motel after this one was dismal, though. And after Eddie showed Jason the hunting knife he carried for self-defense, it seemed they were safe… enough. The white neon letters reading "Motel" on the burgundy-colored sign flickered in the dusky sky as they approached the parking lot, casting more suspicion on their precarious situation. Under any other circumstances, this might have been somewhat amusing. But now it seemed almost mocking in nature.

"At least the 'No Vacancies' sign isn't lit up, too?" Eddie joked.

"I don't think that's *ever* lit up," Jason replied, parking his Mustang.

As both boys stepped out of the car, the silence surrounding them was deafening. All that could be heard over the slight wisp of desert breeze was the buzzing of the antique sign towering above them. Eddie looked up to see a glorious full moon gracing the twilight sky. Nodding toward Jason in jest, "This isn't the part where you turn into a werewolf, is it?"

Jason rolled his eyes and shook his head. "And he can joke at a time like this."

Eddie threw his hands up in defense. "C'mon... it's *funny!*"

"Yeah, funny to *you*. Just... let's go."

Jason opened the screen door to the front office, and they noticed there was no one at the front desk. A round clock hung up on the stark taupe wall behind the desk read 7:30. Jason noticed a bell on the front desk and dinged it with his finger; the sharp trill echoed through the stillness. Both boys pursed their lips and examined the deteriorated surroundings as they waited. The entire room was empty save for a couple worn sofa chairs set against the back wall and a tall faux plant in the corner of the room. Eddie leaned in toward the plant and noticed the large leaves were covered in dust. Cringing, he looked back at Jason and forced a smile, shrugging his shoulders. Jason rolled his eyes and sighed out, resting his elbow on the front desk and leaning his cheek against his fingers. As he rose his hand to tap the bell again, the faint sound of footsteps could be heard from the enclosed hallway to the right of the desk. They scuffed along the floor, dragging with lament it seemed. A crackled voice then boomed from the silence. "Coming! Hold your horses!"

An elderly woman emerged from the long hallway she had just trekked down, facing them now from behind the front desk. She must have been pushing seventy, and seemed oddly elated at the sight of them, revealing a brown, crooked smile with missing teeth. Her thinning gray hair was parted in the middle, lying greasy against petrified skin.

"Evening, boys. Looking to check in for the night, are we?" There was a wet slur in her voice as her tongue wriggled to push against teeth that weren't there.

"Y-yeah," Jason replied. "Just for the night."

"Where you headed in the morning?"

"Oh," Jason scratched his head. "Glad you asked. We're looking to hit I-80. You know how to get there?"

"I-80? Oh, yes." She pointed toward the window to her right, facing the road. "Just take this road north. Take you right to it."

Eddie rubbed his palms together and sighed out in relief, looking next to him at Jason. "Well, ain't *that* a good sign? Finally!"

Jason chuckled and nodded in agreement.

"*Well*, now," the woman spoke again. "Now that we have that cleared up, you're in luck. Just had this one cleaned this morning." Pulling out a drawer from behind the desk, there was a jingling sound as she removed a key from within. With a gnarled, shaking hand, she softly placed it on the countertop before them.

Jason picked it up with slight disgust, wondering what other grimy hands had touched this key. A hint of sorrow then welled inside of him for this poor woman in her debilitated state. That sorrow was replaced with disgust when he unwittingly came in close contact with her face and inhaled breath so putrid his insides churned. She didn't seem to notice his grimace. So far, their cross-country trip was as dead as that breath. Swallowing the lump in his throat, "Thank you. How much for the night?"

"Just twenty dollars."

There was a rustle as Eddie reached into his pocket and procured a wrinkled twenty-dollar bill. He placed it on the desk. "There you go. Thank you, ma'am."

She picked up the crumpled bill and nodded in return. "You're welcome. Enjoy your stay, boys. You need anything at all, just call the front desk."

"Uh... okay," Eddie shrugged, doubtful that she could help with anything.

Jason looked at the ground and nodded, then gazed back at the woman. "We'll be okay, but thanks. Have a nice night."

"You too, boys. G'night."

Eddie pushed open the screen door and they both shuffled out to their room, which was the furthest from the front office, the last one in a long line of paint-stripped blue doors. Once they approached it, Jason glanced at Eddie, pursing his lips and shaking his head. "Here we go." He lodged the key into the keyhole and, upon opening the door and stepping inside, both of their faces cringed in revolt. Stale air hung dank in the motel room, and grimy water stains sprawled across the popcorn ceiling. Each full bed was dressed in the same faded bedding—a peach floral pattern set against moss green. Water droplets dripped from the bathroom faucet in a slow and steady maddening rhythm, and splotchy stains covered the low-pile tan carpet. No surprise, since the outside of the building was just as decrepit.

"It's only for one night," Eddie mumbled.

Jason sighed out and set his backpack down. One night... he could do one night. Looking at his watch, he noticed it was now eight o'clock. Good—they'd leave first thing in the morning. After tossing their backpacks on the beds, they stepped out to get some much-needed fresh air. The sun was beginning to set in the west, coloring the sky with brilliant wisps of violet and orange.

"Would you look at that," Eddie mused. "Quite a sunset."

"Yeah." Jason plopped down in one of the two shabby plastic stack chairs in front of the door, and Eddie sat in the other. Covered in grime, the chairs seemed to mock them. Once bright white, they were now a permanent shade of filth.

Eddie broke the silence. "Well, shit. Seems we've entered the *twilight zone*, haven't we?"

"Sure *have*." Jason shook his head, resting his elbow on his knee and leaning his forehead on his palm. "Eddie... I swear, I was right on track. I don't know *how* the hell we got here."

"It's okay. The skeleton lady who checked us in said to head north, that'll get us to where we want to go. So first thing tomorrow, we head north."

"That lady's disgusting. Did you get a whiff of her breath? Damn, like she ate raw meat or something. Fucking *gross*, man..."

"Nah, I got lucky. Left the check in to you."

Jason shot him a brazen glance, *"Thanks."*

Eddie snickered and waved off his friend's sarcasm. "We just hit a dead zone, that's all. There's lots of 'em out here." Then he reached down to grab his flask placed on the concrete next to his chair and took a swig of whiskey. Gesturing to Jason with the flask, "Want some?"

Pursing his lips and furrowing his brow, Jason took the flask. The rich, smooth liquid instantly relaxed the tension brewing in his body. Next to him, Eddie lit a cigarette and leaned back in his chair, crossing his ankles and resting his hands on his stomach. He looked around them, the empty stretch of road running through untouched desert as far as the eye could see. "Can you imagine living out here? Like, *goddamn!* Shit nothin'."

"Yeah, shit nothin' is right."

Eddie noticed a change in Jason's expression—his friend's eyes suddenly drooped and began to glisten. He nudged Jason's arm. "Thinking about your mom?"

"Yeah..." Jason told Eddie about his mom the first time they got shit drunk together, and Eddie remembered. Someone tells you something like that, you remember, no matter how shit-faced you are.

"Hey, she's in a better place now."

The tears welled in Jason's eyes and began to run down his cheeks. He brushed them away with his forearm, sniffling. "I don't know, man. You know, people like to say that, and... no offense, but... I think it's bullshit."

"None taken."

"It's just... it was too goddamn soon. Sixty-five. She had..." he punched his thigh hard with his fist, "She had so much more life to live. *Fuck* cancer, man."

"Fuck cancer is right. I tell you, life ain't fair. One minute you're livin' on cloud nine, the next... you're facing the fight of your goddamn life."

Just then Jason chuckled.

*"What?"* Eddie asked, confused.

"Just... just thinking about how my mom used to take my friends and me to the arcade when we were little. Just throw us all in the station wagon, drop us off, and come back in a couple hours. She did a lot of stuff like that. She was..." he choked on his words, "She was really fucking amazing, man."

Eddie breathed out slow and turned his gaze to the setting sun, which resembled a sizzling fireball now. "Sounds like your mom was pretty awesome. My mom... yeah, she's great, but... my parents divorced when I was eight. I stayed with her, but she was never home. Got into real estate after the divorce and left me alone most of the time." He laughed and glanced back at Jason. "Don't get me wrong, I had some *killer* parties back in the day, but... would have been nice if she actually stayed around more, you know? Almost like my brother and I were too much of a bother." He looked down and scuffed the concrete with his shoes. "My old man, he wasn't there for me much, either.

So, I kinda just... I don't know... raised *myself* in a way, I guess. My older brother and I... we didn't talk much back then, still don't." After staring into the distance again briefly, he looked back at Jason, who had slumped down in his chair now. "Oh... oh shit. Here I am talkin' all about myself and you don't even *have* your mom anymore."

Jason waved him off. "No, it's fine. We all got our own shit, man. My dad, he's still here, but... he's not, you know? Just glazed eyes. A lost soul... and now *this*." He sat up straight, lifting an arm and moving it in a gesture to showcase their bleak surroundings, "I just wanted to get away from it all, you know? Just... have time to *breathe*. And here we are, in the middle of nowhere. No hot chicks, no good booze..."

"Hey now," Eddie tapped the flask now back in his hand. "This ain't bad, eh?"

Jason chuckled. "Yeah, it ain't bad."

Then Eddie breathed in slow and deep, lifting his head to the sparkling canopy above. "This'll all change, my friend. We're gettin' out of here tomorrow, headin' north to catch the freeway east. I got my sights on Colorado." He turned to Jason. "You ever been skiing there?"

"No, never."

"Ah, that's gonna change. And the snow bunnies?" He snickered, "Let's just say, there's lots of 'em. And boy do they like keepin' you warm."

# 4

## SOMETHING IS BREWING

Eddie awoke the next morning to hazy sunlight filtering through the sheer tan curtains. Jason was still asleep, snoring on the other bed. He had no idea how they'd both been able to sleep in this room the whole night... hell, how they'd been able to sleep at *all*, but he was thankful his hunting knife didn't have to make an appearance. Place like this, he was sure he'd have to brandish that razor-sharp steel at some point.

As his mind often did first thing in the morning, he thought of Angie and how it had all went down. They'd dated for almost a year, up until senior year in college. Then he'd called it off, thinking it was too early to settle down. But now it seemed she was the one that got away. Sweet Angie. Maybe he'd call her up after they got back, see if he still had a chance with her. He still wore the braided leather bracelet she'd bought him, and a slight smile graced his lips as he looked at it now. After a brief reverie, he sat up, eager to shower and wash off whatever muck was lurking in the fibers of these sheets. They felt greasy, and he spied a couple maroon-colored stains in the section he had flung off of him. *What the fuck? We need to get out of this shithole.*

Walking over to the shower, he almost gagged. Black mold crept along the caulk on the bottom, some of it veining upward between the tarnished square white tiles, and it smelled of mildew and cheap cleaner. Shaking his head and biting his lower lip, he reconsidered. There would be a better place to shower later today. He wasn't going to risk getting E. coli for fuck's sake. Just then, he heard Jason stirring. *Thank God.* Walking over to Jason, he smacked him on the head with a pillow, then blurted out, "Get up. We're leaving."

Jason moaned and fluttered his eyes open. "What the *fuck*, man! What... what time is it?"

Eddie leaned over and squinted at Jason's watch on the nightstand. "It's eight." He punched Jason in the shoulder and his friend winced, then began to laugh. "Dude, this isn't funny," Eddie scoffed. "Let's get the fuck outta here. I'm *starving*."

Waving Eddie off, Jason mumbled, "Okay, okay..."

The zombie lady was slumped behind the front counter when they opened the screen door to check out. She lit up in their presence again, greeting them with a roguish smile. In a hoarse voice, she asked, "How was your stay?"

Jason swallowed the lump in his throat. "It was... fine, thanks."

"Wonderful."

As Jason leaned in to give her back the hotel key, he avoided that rancid breath threatening to induce gagging. The woman smiled as the key was dropped into her shriveled hand, and Jason couldn't help feeling a tinge of sadness again for her. What a life, rotting in this decay day after day. After checking out, Eddie asked if there was somewhere they could grab a bite. He and his friend were famished.

"Ah, yes." The woman raised a crooked claw to guide their way; her glassy, bloodshot eyeballs moved slowly to the right as she spoke. Parchment-paper lips crinkled with every word. "Take this road north, on yer way to the freeway. There's a small town a couple miles from here—can't miss it, you'll drive right through. There'll be a diner on the right, before you head in. Best omelets you ever tasted—make sure to get the sausage, it's my favorite," she winked. Then her expression turned grave, and she leaned her frail forearms on the countertop, speaking to them in a whisper. "Just, be careful. There's a *cult*, if you will, on the outskirts of town. Like to *sacrifice* themselves, I hear. Now, I ain't supposed to be *tellin'* you this, but...

just keep on the straight and narrow, ya hear?" She froze for a second as she looked into nothingness and her mouth began to twitch. Jason and Eddie stared at each other, and Eddie mouthed the words, "What the fuck?" Then with a shake of her head, the woman blinked and came to once more. "All I'm sayin' is people tend to go missin' here. You just watch yer steps."

Eddie and Jason exchanged skeptical glances, thanked her, then headed out.

Revving the engine, Jason backed out of the parking lot and headed north. Their growling stomachs beckoned for sustenance as they drove on in a famished daze. "A *cult?* Like... what the *fuck?* You think that loony knows what she's talking about? And what the hell *happened* to her in there?" Jason said as he blinked his eyes, fighting off incoming delirium. "I don't know, man. I can't take much more of this. We're in la-la land out here. And you think there's really a diner serving *legit* food in this hellhole?"

"Shit, I'll just about believe *anyone* at this point if they say there's good food nearby. And cult or no cult, I don't fuckin' care." Eddie brushed off the idea. "There ain't no cult. She's just batshit crazy. I know I could eat a goddamn *horse* right now, though! Hell, I might even try that sausage omelet."

Jason grimaced, "That's *disgusting*. What you wanna bet there's human meat in those omelets?"

Eddie shrugged. "Protein is protein." Then, after a minute or two of silence, the diner sign came into view—on the right, just as the woman had promised. "Would you look at that? Old bag hasn't lost her marbles after all!"

The large metal letters adorning the sign read "Diner" and were a lackluster coral green. Rust had begun to eat at the metal, revealing random splotches of brown. The gas-discharge tubes running the length of each letter were most likely vacuous at this point, and each letter sat atop a long, thin metal base. The base itself had succumbed to extreme deterioration as well, with dark brown and brick red shades of rust taking over.

Jason pursed his lips and chirped rhetorically, "Well, isn't *this* welcoming?!" Pulling his Mustang into the vacant parking lot, he cut the engine. The morning sunlight reflected hard from the glass windows of the diner, which was painted a tarnished white. He and Eddie strained their eyes to see inside. There was a person behind the counter serving coffee and they could make out a couple customers sitting in booths.

Eddie opened his door first, looking at Jason as he did so. "C'mon, how bad can it be?"

Jason shook his head and opened his door, following his friend in. A door chime rang their arrival, and the lady behind the counter looked up from the cash register. The sunlight pouring in through the windows illuminated her smooth brown skin, and she greeted them with a beautiful smile. It was a welcome sight, in stark contrast to the bent smile that had sent them off this morning. She must have been mid-forties. "Morning, and welcome. Please..." she motioned toward the empty booth before her. "Take a seat, I'll be right with ya." She handed them both plastic menus, and they walked a bit apprehensively toward the booth. "Don't worry, I don't bite," she joked with a sugary voice. The boys both feigned a mock chuckle, then took their seats.

"Doesn't something seem *off* to you?" Jason whispered to Eddie. "Like, maybe that old lady was right about that cult shit."

"I don't know, I mean... rundown town, away from much civilization. Seems normal, really. Let's just eat breakfast and get outta here."

Jason eyed the menu with reluctance, ignoring the disquiet slowly creeping up inside him, and played along. After a few minutes, the lady waltzed over to their booth with her notepad in hand, ready to take their order.

"Have we decided yet, gentlemen?"

Eddie piped up first, "I'll try the sausage omelet, heard that's a good one." Jason shot him a disgusted look.

"Best around, if ya ask me," she chimed, scrawling his order down. Then she nodded her head toward Jason.

"I'll… I'll get the sunnyside breakfast, eggs scrambled. And can we have two coffees, please?"

"Coming right up." She winked as she took their menus from them and briskly walked off. Jason cleared his throat, looking around them. The faded powder blue vinyl upholstering lining the booth they sat in was cracking throughout, exposing the cream-colored foam within. Silver flakes speckled the white laminate finish of the retro dining table—they were silent observers to his unease this morning. The black-and-white checkered tiles lining the floor had caught his interest as soon as they'd walked in, and now he noticed how awfully discolored they were.

Resting his elbows on the countertop, Jason leaned in, wanting to address these red flags with Eddie. An eerie sound prevented him from speaking, though. They both heard it—the indistinguishable noise of something heavy sliding along the ceramic tiles. Jason looked over Eddie's shoulder to see an older man, probably mid-sixties, walking to their booth. He stopped next to them and looked down with cracked lips that spread into a cursory smile. Age and experience had worn deep grooves across his forehead, and he wore thick-lensed glasses that magnified his shallow blue eyes. A few wisps of greasy black hair were combed to the side of his head.

In a raspy voice, the man spoke. "You fellas lost? Got that look written all over yer faces."

Eddie nodded his head, sporting a smile with pursed lips. "You read faces well. We *were* lost, but... back on track now."

"Is that right? Well, good to hear. Lots of folks get lost here, mind you. Bermuda Triangle of the desert, you could say."

Jason eyed him with trepidation. "Yeah, I can see that. Heading north after this, catch the freeway and be back on track."

"North, you say. Oh, goodness. Give yourself a treat on the way and stop by Jade's place, just outside 'a town. Best psychic around, I tell you. Don't know where she gets it from, but, what a gift." He paused, then continued with a wink, "Easy on the eyes, too."

Jason chuckled under his breath. "Thanks, but... not much of a believer in the whole *psychic realm*." He used air quotes as he spoke the last two words.

The older man bowed his head, showcasing the black hair straggling across parched, sallow flesh. "To each their own." Then he stood as straight as he could, which wasn't much. The hump rounding his back was relentless. "Well, enjoy your breakfast. Best this side of the desert. And safe travels..."

As he turned to walk away, there was the sound of something heavy again dragging along the tiles. Jason and Eddie stared at each other, perplexed. Then they lowered their gaze to the man's feet, and realized he had no feet at all. What he had instead were slabs of concrete poorly strapped to the bottom of each leg. Thick leather straps ran up his legs from each slab, attached by nail heads to the outer and inner sides of the concrete. They disappeared under his soiled, flooded tan trouser pants, their destination unknown. They both gawked at each other, speechless.

While their minds were trying to comprehend the horror they'd just witnessed, the waitress cheerily walked over with two coffees. "Here you go, boys." She couldn't miss Jason's implausible stare as he followed the debilitated old man's laborious journey back to his booth. Glancing briefly at the man, she then looked back to Jason. "Oh, Fred? Yeah, can give newcomers the creeps." Leaning in to them both, cupping one hand around her mouth, she whispered, "Says he had a run-in with the *devil* a ways back. Devil took his feet." Then she shrugged, glancing toward Fred again, "Don't know what to think about *that*, but... *Lordy*, is he in some state of hell now."

Turning to face them both, she then donned a bright smile, the corners of her mouth playfully curving upward. "Food'll be right up, boys. Can tell you poor fellas are *hungry!*" With a sunny wink, she whisked herself away, leaving Jason and Eddie pondering what evil indeed lurked in the dark seams of this grim Bermuda Triangle they had stumbled into.

# 5

## Car Trouble

Both boys walked back to Jason's car after eating a surprisingly delicious breakfast they no doubt surmised would poison them, succumbing them to the bowels of this barren wasteland. As they did so, each glanced to their right at the town. It was really just a few rugged buildings. One faded white building had a weathered wooden steeple perched atop, and the others weren't discernible. Could be small businesses—though how could those thrive out here? How the hell could a diner thrive out here—and a *motel* for that matter? They were stumped, but had no desire to explore this unsettling dust bowl anymore.

As they stepped into the red Mustang, Jason turned the key in the ignition to start the engine. Nothing. He tried it again... still nothing. "What the absolute—" Jason's thought was cut short by the sight of Fred, slowly lurching toward them, the concrete blocks strapped to his ankles drawing deep grooves in the dirt. Eddie was staring at the man with absolute dread.

"Um, *Jason?* Gonna get this car started?"

"I'm *trying!* There's no reason it shouldn't start now. *None!*"

Jason kept pressing the gas pedal and turning the key, all the while looking up through the windshield at the lumbering man continuing toward them.

"What the fuck is his *problem?*" Eddie chided. "Dude's a living nightmare... what the hell does he want with—" Just then, Jason jumped as there was a knock on the driver's side window. Looking to his left, his eyes met those of a beautiful girl who seemed to be around their age. Her messy brown hair was pulled up into a ponytail, and soft bangs graced her forehead. Sparkling blue eyes curved up at the edges as she smiled sweetly. Jason looked toward Eddie, who shrugged and shook his head, eyes wide. "I mean, she looks pretty normal to *me*. I think she's safe." They both then looked toward the old man, who had stopped in his tracks now, and was staring almost absentmindedly at them.

Jason manually rolled his window down. "H-hi?"

"Hey!" She greeted them cheerfully. "Trouble with your car, huh? Listen... there's a car shop just outside 'a town. They're fixing my car right now. One sec..." She fished something out of the pocket of her jean shorts, her hand popping back up with a small card clasped between her fingers. "Here... here's their number."

Eddie looked at her, puzzled. "What happened to *your* car?"

"I was on my way here, just outside of town, and... car broke down. Started *smokin'!* Lucky for me, the shop's tow truck was passing by. Took my car to the shop. It might be a few days, part's gotta come in and all, but..." she shrugged, "What do you do?"

"Why would someone like *you* come through this town?" Jason asked. "You don't..." he looked to the old man now, who had turned around and was headed back into the diner, "Well, you don't *look* like someone who'd be passing through."

"I have my reasons, same as you." Then she slapped her hands on the top edge of the car door, leaning low to look at them both. "Hey, good luck with your car. I'm gonna do some explorin'. Don't you just love towns like this? A relic from the past."

"Uh, I *guess*," Jason managed to respond.

"Well, see ya!" she waved as she walked off, her backpack bouncing with each zesty step. A boy was waiting for her, and he put his arm around her waist as they walked away. Must have been her boyfriend.

Jason and Eddie looked at each other, trying to comprehend what the hell just happened. Sighing,

Jason lifted the card, staring at the number. He then noticed the pay phone in front of the diner. Looking at Eddie, "You think this is rigged? You think someone did this to my car on *purpose?* The fact that her car just broke down, too—right here?" He shook his head. "This is fucked up, man. Feels like we're living a goddamn horror movie. I got an uneasy feeling. I don't like this."

He stepped out and popped the hood. After a close inspection revealed nothing awry, Jason had no other choice but to call the tow truck company. Shortly after, the driver arrived in an antique Dodge tow truck, the original blue paint eaten away by voracious rust. He stood well above six feet, sporting some mean Wolverine mutton chops. A soiled red bandana donned his head, and he wore weathered denim suspenders over a grimy white T-shirt. To say he was menacing was an understatement. After the man gruffly told them they'd be hearing from him, the boys watched as he hooked up Jason's beloved Mustang to the tow and drove off. According to him, they could stay at the motel (that awful pigsty) until the car was fixed. Depending on the issue, it might take a few days.

As they both watched the truck drive away, Eddie nudged Jason in the arm. "Hey, want your fortune told?"

"What? Pfft, *no!* That's literally the *last* thing on my mind right now."

"Aww, c'mon! Dude, that guy said she's hot." He shrugged his shoulders. "I mean, just sayin'. *Jade?* Sounds hot to me."

Jason rolled his eyes. "No! That shit's stupid. They tell everyone the same thing. Everyone has a dead relative, hopes at a promotion, some... fucking idea they have they've been too scared to do. It's not hard to find something and run with it."

"You want to go back to the motel, then?"

"No..." Jason threw his hands up in defeat. "*Fine!* Fine. Let's go find... Jade. Have her tell us all our wildest dreams are about to come true."

Eddie slapped his back. "See! And what if they are?" He wiggled his fingers and sported a ridiculous smile, his eyes wide.

"You're pathetic."

***

Though the scorching sun was high in the sky, the lack of humidity made their walk tolerable. Jason and Eddie scuffed along, not saying much, both knowing there was a real chance they might never get out of this godforsaken town. The human arm, the guy with concrete slabs for feet, the car engine suddenly not turning over. A fucking *cult*. It all seemed to fit together now, a sick running joke. Once they were about a half mile out of town, Eddie spoke up, childlike excitement in his voice. "Jason. Dude! There it is! Holy shit. And Jade looks hot as *fuck*, man."

Jason looked to where Eddie was pointing, off to the right, and saw a woman sitting on a distressed wooden chair outside of a small shack. The dark wood planks of the shack were weathered, showing signs of age. Faded yellow words were painted across the wood in front, right under the sagging roofline. They read, "Jade's Psychic Readings". Painted sporadically around the words were yellow starbursts. Oddly enough, a pay phone stood in front of the shack. Not a high-traffic area, but he had grown accustomed to accepting that nothing out here made a fuckton of sense.

Jason's eyes then fell on an ankle-length woman's black leather boot that was casually rocking up and down. Looking up further, the bare ivory skin of a long and lean leg began to show, crossed over another. The skin continued on, revealing taut thighs visible between the slit of a long, sheer black dress. Wavy red hair cascaded softly down to waist level, some brazen strands adorning an ample bust. Exposed slender shoulders rose up and down as the woman leaned forward, her forearms resting on her thighs. A soft oval face greeted them, green eyes sparkling with a hint of mischief under feathered bangs.

"Howdy, boys." Her voice was sultry and sweet.

"Uh... howdy... *yourself*," Jason managed to sputter out.

"J-Jade?" Eddie asked.

She sat up straight and cocked her head, her fingers softly wrapping around her knees. "Yes. Who's asking?"

"This is my buddy, Jason." Eddie pointed to him. "And I'm... Eddie."

"Well, it's mighty nice to *meet* you, boys. Let me guess, townsfolk sent you here? *Fred*, perhaps?"

"Um, yeah," Jason answered. "Said you're the best around. And, listen," he raised his palms up as if under arrest. "I'm not into this, whole, *psychic* stuff. No offense. But my *friend*, here. Well, he said we might as well pay you a visit. My car's in the shop right now, so..."

She looked Eddie straight in the eyes and he fought a hard-on. "I see. Eddie, your heart is pure. Your intuition... uncanny. You were right to come here. There are events in your future you both must know. Events..." she stood up slowly. "I can reveal to you." At this, both Jason and Eddie swallowed hard, the blood rushing between their legs.

"Please, come in," she said with a graceful wave of her hand. "Let me read for you. I sense a bright future for you both. You have so much... potential."

Looking at Jason, Eddie shrugged. "I mean, why not?"

Though Jason felt slight perturbation, he followed his friend into Jade's shack. As he did so, he couldn't help but notice the large building off in the distance. Strange, such a building out here, with no windows to be seen. Had to be abandoned. Dark curiosity piqued as he furrowed his brows, stepping into the soft glow of candlelight.

# 6

## Meat for the Master

He had been born into darkness and would die in the darkness, just like the rest of them. It was all they had ever known... that and the taste of sweet, raw human flesh.

Their master had been here since the dawn of time, and they were servants to his insatiable appetite for pain and destruction. He had taken their voices from them, and in return they followed his every command. Many had been before him, and many would follow after he perished.

Sometimes he wondered how long he'd been alive. Gazing at his own skin now, he noticed how sallow it was; simply a fleshy casing which held the decadent meat within. The veins pumping life blood through his body were clearly visible—indigo lines sprawling underneath pallor flesh. Then he heard her whimper. They always whimpered... every last one of them. It came before the screams.

He crouched down in front of her, and a snarl spread across his face as he lifted his head to meet her terrified gaze. She was slumped against the concrete wall, every inch of her shaking in fear. He could smell it now, that delicious aroma... a mix of sweat and adrenaline. Resting his forearms on his flexed thighs, he cocked his head and opened his mouth, smiling wide.

And just like all the others, she screamed in hysteria when she saw the stump of his tongue squirm in his damp mouth.

***

She was being led by her captors into a dark, concrete room. The scant light from the flickering candles adorning the floor lit her way, and a large device stood at the far end of the room against the wall, in the upside-down shape of a bell. A man's face graced the top of it, and his mouth was agape in torment. The device looked to be very heavy, possibly made of steel. Buttons ran down the length of it in vertical lines, and two handles were visible on its visage.

She couldn't see the faces of her captors, but could hear their primitive grunts as they forced her toward this odd device. Placing the heels of her bare feet hard against the cold concrete floor, she tried with all her might to push against them and delay this inevitable grim procession. But it was no use... she felt weak against their vice grips and her entire body ached, as if she had been starved and beaten. They were only a few feet away from the device now, and a hooded figure stepped forward from behind them and stood directly in front of it. With both hands, he grabbed the handles and opened two doors wide, then stepped to the side and clasped his hands in front of him.

With the inside exposed, she realized now that it was an iron maiden. Spikes that were several inches long lined the inside, their sharp points gleaming in the soft candlelight. She fought against the steel grasp of her captors with all her might, shaking her head wildly as jagged screams tore up her throat and raged into the stark expanse of this dungeon. No one would come to her aid, though, she was sure of it. How had it come to this? How had she gotten here? Her body was turned in a violent manner so that her back now faced the device. She could make out their faces now... hollow eyes stared at her, void of any humanity. Almost animalistic in nature.

She was being pushed backward into the device now, and as those first few spikes pierced her backside, the pain was already excruciating. Though she struggled to escape the sheer torture penetrating her entire backside, she could feel the rusty iron spears slowly penetrating her every limb and encroaching upon her internal organs. Her vision began to wane as the spikes piercing her brain took hold. Then, as her body was lodged inside, the room began to disappear as both doors closed in on her, entombing her within. The interior of each door was laden with a series of spikes even longer in length and, once again, they began to puncture her flesh, this time piercing through the front of her body. A scream formed in the back of her throat as darkness fell on her. Unable to move, she fought to force it out. But the spikes, the spikes had skewered her entire head now and—

Carrie woke up in a cold sweat, gasping for breath. She lifted her hands to feel every inch of her body, making sure she was in one piece. The nightmare had been so vivid, so sinister. Closing her eyes, she inhaled slow and exhaled slower, a method she had learned once during a meditation class. It slowed the heart rate down, and soon her rapid heartbeat began to normalize. How she had even been able to fall asleep in this darkened tomb was astonishing, and her back was now aching. Even though she'd stuffed her hoodie between her back and the wall for cushioning, it had done little to buffer the hard surface.

Pulling her knees to her chest, she then wrapped her arms around her legs, which helped to alleviate some of the pain. Once she had her breathing under control, she fought to calm her racing mind. Panicking right now would only ensure a miscalculation, which could be deadly. As she sat in the darkness, finally in control of her mindset, she pondered her choices. The fortuity of her preparation for this endeavor did not escape her. She'd packed leg wrap (now wrapped well around her ankle), a few snacks, water, and other essentials. But the food and water wouldn't last. She had a day or two before her rations would run out completely. For now, thanks to the unavoidable rest she faced lurking in the shadows, at least her ankle was feeling better.

She couldn't believe her own beguiling. She and her friends were always daring each other, and Kristy had really struck a nerve when she'd told Carrie she was too chickenshit to step foot in this town. Because when people did, they almost always disappeared. So, what did Carrie do? Of course, she vowed to prove Kristy wrong. And now, it had quite possibly meant a death sentence. *Curiosity killed the cat... Curiosity killed the Carrie.* She clenched her eyes shut and shook her head, trying desperately to calm the hurricane of tormented thoughts threatening to wreak havoc again on her composed state.

The kid had tricked her. While she was driving into town, just past some deteriorated shack, she had spied a scruffy little boy off to the right, waving his lanky arms and screaming. Putting her car in park and turning off the engine, she'd grabbed her backpack and walked briskly to the boy, anxious to help in any way she could. Should have known it was a trap. She followed this innocent little thing to his mom, who was lying on the ground, looking as pale as a ghost. In fact, they both were deathly pale. That should have been the first sign something was awry. Out in this scorching desert with nary a touch of sun? Wasn't logical.

She surmised she was lurking in the nest of some sort of cult. After the man had been sawed to death, she'd heard the wet sound of chewing, and it took all of her willpower not to retch right then and there. There was the sound of fingers scrawling the concrete, tissue being torn, and even small bones being snapped. *Christ... Goddamn cannibals.* She was a horror movie fanatic, but the whole point was she was always behind a *screen*. To be *living* this? It was incomprehensible fear and adrenaline. Fight or flight, but her only option now was... *stay*. She would dare to explore more of this clammy concrete dungeon at the right time, to find an exit, and thankfully her energy to fuck shit up was returning. Carrie had taken martial arts classes since she was a kid up until her senior year of college, just three years ago. She kept a trim, muscular physique. But martial artist versus cannibal cultists? Could swing either way, and she wasn't sure how many of them were lurking within. She had heard female voices during the feeding, though, so at least there were some she could most definitely overpower.

All was quiet now, and she flicked the flashlight on to illuminate her watch. Ten o'clock. Should she dare explore at this point? Would they all be sleeping? Ever so slowly, she moved her right foot. It hit a bone, the clatter echoing off the walls of the concrete chamber she sought refuge in. She waited. Nothing... Did they know her location? Were they silently mocking her, waiting in the shadows, salivating over what she would taste like? This sent her mind into horrifying overdrive. Because she was a woman, maybe they wouldn't want to kill her right away. Maybe they would want to keep her for... She shook her head, clearing the thought from her mind. *Focus, Carrie.*

Slowly standing to a crouch, she pushed her shoulders back and raised her head upward. Stretching in this tomb of a space was practically impossible, but she had to get the blood flowing somehow. She grabbed the lightweight black hoodie from the floor and threw it on over her gray tank top. Removing the elastic from her wrist, she wrapped her long, thick black hair into a ponytail. Placing her small flashlight and her pocketknife into the pockets of her tan cargo pants, she put her hands on the flat bottom surface of one of the arched openings and slowly guided her body out. Her tank top was soiled with sweat, and more than ever she could feel the coolness of the fabric against her skin. Slowly zipping up her hoodie, warmth returned.

Turning to the right, she instinctively covered her nose with the back of her hand and furrowed her brows. The putrid stench was overwhelming from outside the crawlspace she had been hiding in. Before proceeding any farther, she stood still, listening for any sounds. Still nothing. She crept forward slowly, each careful step barely making a sound. A few candles were still burning on the floor, and a dim light bulb flickering from the ceiling at the back of the room cast eerie shadows along the smooth stone surfaces.

The lighting illuminated the cold, gleaming metal that comprised the large circular device. It was in the center of an otherwise empty and windowless concrete room—a menacing presence looming over her. She noticed four cuffs attached to the edges, where hands and feet would naturally be locked in, that were covered in maroon stains. And under the device, lying on the floor before her, were the remnants of human organs, some still glistening in the candlelight. Bile began pushing its way up her throat, but she fought it back. It would only wake the others, ensuring *her* glistening organs would be next.

A thin groove in the concrete flooring revealed the razor-sharp teeth of a massive saw. Bits of meat still clung to the decrepit metal teeth. *What the...? Who* are *these demented fucks?* Looking toward the back of the room, she noticed another stairwell leading up. Maybe this led to an exit? She'd already fallen about ten feet, and that was on concrete. Falling ten feet onto the earth at least provided a softer impact and the opportunity to roll into a running start. Swallowing hard and steeling herself, she quietly walked toward the stairwell and began ascending the steps, which wrapped in a spiral within the concrete walls.

Soft light flooded the stairwell as she approached the next floor. With pocketknife in hand, she pulled the black hood over her head and knelt on the steps, peering slightly over the top step—enough to take in the scene before her. It was a large rectangular room. Mold ran up the concrete walls, glowing a soft shade of violet. A narrow, smooth stone table practically ran the length of the room, and a chair made of human bones sat at each end. The backs of the chairs towered a few feet high, and human skulls were mounted along the top of each. Standing at one end of the table on the far right were four hooded figures. Brown robes covered their entire bodies, and they stood still with their hands clasped in front of them. Their hands resembled claws and long, sharp fingernails protruded from each fingertip. Carrie could barely make out the bottoms of their faces, but found no expression.

They were all staring at the other side of the table. It seemed something large was sitting in the opposite chair. She couldn't quite discern any details, but did notice what looked like thick, spiraled horns. Behind the chair glowed an arched portal of some kind—it was deep red in color, and the murky edges pulsated. The hooded figures continued to stand still as a bright light lit up in the back wall to the right of them, revealing a thick slate of glass. Behind the glass were two narrow concrete slabs running from the floor to the ceiling. Then she heard it—a long, terrifying scream. The scream of a woman. It grew ever so louder, lamenting anguish. Carrie's heart was a hammer now, relentlessly pounding in her chest. Her eyes widened with terror and she began to tremble.

The screams became muffled as a naked woman slowly slid down behind the glass through an opening in the top. Her agonizing screams, barely audible behind the glass, tore from her throat as she violently shook her head back and forth. She was somehow able to raise her palms in the tight space and place them in front of her against the glass. There was no bottom that Carrie could see—the tight enclosure seemed to hold her in place. She remained in this position for a few seconds, then a loud motor sound erupted as pistons pushed the concrete slabs slowly toward her. The woman looked left and right frantically, trying with all her might to somehow push her body up, but it was futile. Carrie hunched her shoulders and drew a deep breath in, staring in utter horror. Just as it seemed the woman would be crushed, the slabs halted to a stop. Silence ensued, and all Carrie could hear was her own heavy breathing. She placed her palm over her mouth to quiet the sound.

The sharp metal sound of spinning saws ripped through the silence now. Several small circular saw blades rose up from the bottom of the glass enclosure, visible from within the concrete slab they were nestled in. Their teeth spun violently, and glistening tears could be seen on the woman's face. Her despondent eyes, searching the darkness, somehow found Carrie crouching on the steps. And for a few terrifying seconds, Carrie unknowingly locked eyes with the once-sprightly young woman who had stopped to offer Jason and Eddie help with their car. The woman who had a smile like sunshine and an effervescent zest for life. And when the sharp metal blades tore into her toes, ripping her feet to shreds, the woman's mouth shot open and she arched her head up. Blood splattered against the inside of the glass enclosure as the saws continued to grind farther up. Her gut-wrenching screams became weaker within the glass tomb, now covered with blood and bits of meat.

Carrie's breathing was hard and fast, her heart frantically pumping to allow for a swift escape, but she was fixated on the macabre scene before her. Every muscle in her body was on high alert, paralyzed by electrifying fear. The frenzied sound of spinning metal finally came to a stop. The glass remained lit, however. In the heavy silence that blanketed the room, her racing pulse throbbed in her head. Though she could no longer see through the gore-covered glass, she assumed the woman had to be dead. No sound emanated from the glass tomb. She closed her eyes and, as warm tears dripped to her bare knees, sent a prayer to the woman behind the glass. Her torture was finally over. Bile began to work its way up her throat as she thought about the gruesome scene that had just played out before her. Saws ripping into live flesh, the torturous screams of a woman being sawed to death. Covering her mouth with the back of her hand, she hunched over and again fought the burning acid back down.

The mold in the room glowed brighter now and began to throb. As Carrie carefully placed her right hand on the step below her and moved her right foot to begin descending the stairwell, she saw a small glass tube light up on the foreside of the glass enclosure. It was no larger in circumference than a couple inches.

A bright red, curdled liquid began to pass through the tube, and she realized this was the meat from the woman in the enclosure. Her shredded meat, resembling chum now, was being pushed through. *What the fuck is this sick shit?!* The tube ran the length of the table, its illumination showcasing the flow of fresh human meat. And just as it approached the looming bone chair on the left side of the room, the tube curved directly upward. As it did so, the dark figure she had barely discerned before bent down to receive the food from it. The light from both the glass enclosure and the bright mold softly illuminated its features, and her stare lingered on its form. Once she came to grips with the reality of what she was looking at, sheer terror consumed her.

It wasn't human—it was some kind of... *demon*. Taut skin stretched the length of its body, with flesh shredded in parts. The skin itself was a purplish red—the color of a fresh bruise—and it glistened in the soft light. It was also so thin she could make out the scrawling veins and fibrous muscles underneath. It seemed to have no eyes—simply large, empty sockets. Void of any expression, it was simply a fiend ready to feed. But the mouth was hideous! A gutted black hole in the middle of its face, it was lined with serrated teeth. As the meat entered the end of the tube, the beast leaned its hideous head forward and suction-cupped its gaping maw to the glass device. Carrie could hear the sick sound of it sucking the meat in, and she covered her mouth in disgust.

She had to get out of here, and fast. With palms placed firmly on the third-highest concrete step, she slowly lowered her right foot to the step below and followed with her left foot. She'd only descended three steps when the sounds of a faint thump and a man screaming erupted from below—no saws, though. Was it safe to run? She had no choice. When scuffling was heard from the demon room above, she took this chance to run like hell down those stairs and not look back.

Maybe someone else had fallen in... Maybe now she had help.

# 7

## Gotcha

Jade sat opposite Jason and Eddie at a small table in the center of the shack. The flames atop the two white pillar candles on both sides of her appeared to dance in mock jubilation. With a demure smile, she leaned forward and rested her forearms on the table, placing one delicate hand on top of the other. Dark purple-colored nails adorned each long finger, and she smelled of sweet, musky vanilla.

"So, boys, what'll it be?"

Eddie gulped, hoping she was referring to something other than a reading. "W-what do you *mean?*"

She chuckled playfully and then leaned back, swiping the soft, long locks of red hair that hung over her bust behind her right shoulder. Jason flushed and briefly looked away, but Eddie ogled her every graceful movement. "*You* know what I mean," she replied. The two boys looked at each other in confusion, then Eddie grinned. "The reading, sillies!" And just like that, the grin left his face.

"Well..." Jason replied. "What kind of readings do you *do?*"

"I do tarot card readings and palm readings." She rested one elbow on the table, nestled her chin in her palm, and stroked the top of Jason's hand with a delicate finger. Jason pulled his hand back reflexively, and she seemed to revel in his shyness.

"How much?" Eddie asked.

"Hmm..." she mused, looking up with a finger to her chin. "For you two, no charge."

*"Really?"* Eddie asked, surprised. "Why no charge?"

"Well, let's just say I have the feeling you boys have been through a hell of a lot. It's written all over your faces."

"Uh, yeah... 'Bout sums it up," Eddie replied, leaning back in his chair and cocking his head.

"A palm reading!" Jason blurted out, instantly regretting his enthusiasm once Eddie smirked at him.

"Well, would you look at that?" Jason sneered at Eddie's sarcastic comment. "Not one for the psychic realm, or so I *thought*."

"Not one for *tarot* cards."

"Well, then. A palm reading it is." Jade sat up straight, placing her hands on the table, palms face up, and studied them both with piercing green eyes. "Who's first?"

Jason gestured to Eddie. "You go first... Your idea to come here, anyway."

"Oh, I'll *gladly* do the honors." Lifting his chin up, Eddie smirked as he outstretched his arms and placed his hands palms up on hers. She gazed at him, the corners of her lips curling upward ever so slightly, then began to hum a sweet melody as her eyes scanned the lines sprawling along the flesh of his hands.

"Interesting..."

"Why, what do you see?" Eddie asked.

"Well. Your head line... that's this one here." She used a pointer finger to trace the line that ran along the middle of his right palm. "On both hands, it's forked and curves upward. A sign you have the talent of communication, and you're pretty good at adapting to new situations. Which I've already seen." She shot him a curt smile. "Your heart line, though. Hmm..."

*"What?"*

"I see you are quite the Casanova."

Eddie laughed and stared at the floor for a second, then bit his lower lip and met her gaze again. Lifting a hand, he ruffled his scruffy, dark blond hair. "I suppose the ladies would call me that."

Jade smirked, then went on. "Your heart line... it's broken. Not one for commitment?"

"If I found the right *girl*, I would be."

The air was getting thick, and Jason could feel the attraction between Eddie and Jade. It sizzled as it magnified, leaving him the odd man out. Furrowing his brow, he kicked Eddie in the leg.

"What the *hell*, bro?!"

Jason politely nodded toward Jade. "Can we get on with it?"

"Oh," she responded, flustered. "Of course." Sitting up straight, she closed her eyes, then opened them as if she were seeing everything in a whole new light. "Well, onto my favorite." She glanced at Eddie gravely. "Your life line."

Eddie cleared his throat and adjusted his posture in the chair, exchanging a brief, uncomfortable glance with Jason. The sound of her voice had left them both anxious, and this fun little charade was beginning to feel foreboding. Then Eddie shook his head, sighing out, and gave her the go-ahead. "Hit me."

She chuckled under her breath. "You two are taking this *way* too literally. A short life line doesn't suggest an early death." She waved their unease off with a flick of her hand. "I'm just messin' with ya. However... a broken *life* line, that's an interesting one. And... yours break on both hands. See?" With her pointer fingers, she gracefully traced the life lines on both of his hands.

"So what does that mean? That I'm gonna—" There was a loud trill as the pay phone began to ring out front, and Jade clapped her hands together.

"Oh, this is good news, boys!" She stood up and rushed outside in an excited frenzy, leaving them both completely perplexed. Both of them could hear her speaking to the person on the other end of the line, but couldn't make out any words.

Jason eyed Eddie and shook his head, rolling his eyes. "C'mon, dude. This is *stupid*. She's been toying with us this whole time. Fuckin'... Let's just go back. I don't wanna deal with this shit anymore." Eddie was just about to beg to differ when Jade came waltzing back in, rubbing her palms together in elation. She cocked her head to the side and sported a dazzling smile.

"Guys..." She lifted her arms up high. "You're free!"

Eddie squinted his eyes in confusion. "Um... *free?*"

"Yes! That was the shop calling—they call this number often when we have out-of-towners who have ventured over to see *moi*." With this, she curtsied. "They can't find you in town? Well... probably at Jade's place, then."

"So they... My car. Is it fixed?" Jason asked.

"Yes! Not that I'm happy to see you both go. Especially *you*." She booped Eddie's nose. Her zest was rather odd, and it cast a shadow over their enthusiasm. But Jason wasted no time, and abruptly stood up.

"Well, shit! I guess it's farewell for now, huh?" He eyed Eddie, who was still staring at Jade, his mouth agape with bewilderment. Jabbing his friend in the shoulder with his elbow, Jason repeated himself. *"Huh?"*

"Oh, yeah. I guess, but..." Eddie eased himself out of his chair, as if any rash move would ruin the moment even more. "My *life* line. You didn't finish my reading."

"Oh, sweetie." She stood in front of him and placed her hands on his shoulders, staring at him with those brilliant green eyes. "You will go on to do great things. Trust me, I can see it. So much potential." Then she took his rough hands in hers and gently kissed his forehead. Jason just stood there, watching this scene play out as if he were an outsider looking in. This girl creeped him out. Sure, she was fuckin' hot. But she reeked hella crazy, and he wanted out of here.

"Where is the shop?" Jason blurted out.

Releasing Eddie's hands, Jade walked out of the shack and they followed behind her. Using her right hand as a visor, she stared into the distance and pointed. "See that building over there? Shop's right on the other side, can't miss it." It was the building Jason had glimpsed before they had headed in here for...

whatever the hell had just transpired. The ominous building with no windows. A lump suddenly formed in his throat, and he gulped it down with unease. She noticed his trepidation and addressed it. "Only about a mile walk, not even. Won't take you guys long. Besides, sun's still high... Not getting dark anytime soon."

Jason sighed and looked at Eddie, who was realizing that nothing more would come out of this. His Casanova ways had led nowhere this time. "C'mon, man. We gotta get outta here." He then looked at Jade. "It was nice meeting you. And good luck with... well, *shit*. With *this*." Upon speaking that last word, he gestured to the barrenness surrounding them. "Sure hope you get outta here one day."

"Oh, I'm happy where I am. This is where I'm supposed to be. It's all for a higher purpose." With that, she winked at him. Jason just shook his head, confounded, and started walking toward the building in the distance.

Eddie begrudgingly backtracked as he stayed in line with Jason and waved to Jade with forlorn. "Was fun while it lasted. Wish it would have lasted longer." She waved back and blew him a kiss. That was the last time they ever saw Jade.

***

Eddie kicked at the dirt like a stubborn toddler as they walked on. "Dude... She was so *hot!*"

"A hot *mess.*"

"I dunno, man. She's the hottest thing we've seen since we got here. Besides that girl back in town, the one who told us about the shop. She was pretty cute."

"We are on to way hotter girls, man. Once we're outta this shithole."

Eddie pondered Jason's words and nodded his head in agreement, grimacing and shrugging his shoulders. "You ain't *wrong.*" Then he gazed upon the building they were closing in on, its menacing visage becoming more distinguishable the closer they got. "What the hell kind of building is this, *anyway?* No windows? Like... what the fuck?"

"I don't know, man. This whole town is a goddamn twilight zone. And, yet again—I don't feel right. Something's off, man." They were very close to the building now, yet there was no sign of a car shop anywhere. The exterior was weathered gray concrete, and most of it had succumbed to dark green mold. It looked to be about three stories high, but was hard to discern with the absence of windows. "Who the hell built this—" The anguished scream of a woman tore through the silence surrounding them. It was frantic and sharp, cutting through the balmy air.

"Please! *Please!!* Help me!" The boys turned to where the scream came from, and saw a woman kneeling on the ground cradling a young child. The woman wore a long, flowing white dress, and her ratty black hair was pulled into a messy ponytail. "Please! You have to *help* me! My baby... my *baby!!*" She rocked back and forth on her knees, pressing her forehead to the child's cheek. The child she was holding was a little boy—looked to be about six years old. They wasted no time and ran to the woman in distress. Eddie pulled in front of Jason, and just as he was about to reach the woman, he fell into the earth.

Jason stopped in his tracks, trying to comprehend what had just happened. The sound of Eddie calling his name sprung him back into action, and he slid onto his stomach to look below. Eddie had fallen into some kind of a trap. A damn hole in the ground, but not just *any* hole. Jason could make out steps ascending from one side of it, and a dark tunnel on the other. He reached his hand down to grab his friend's outstretched hand, but suddenly Eddie was covered in countless writhing limbs. They slithered over him, reaching and grabbing until he was dragged into the dark tunnel, screaming Jason's name. All that was left was his flask of whiskey and his lighter—they had both been jostled from his back pocket during the fall. No knife, but that meant Eddie still had it—at least he hoped so. As his heart beat like a hammer, Jason considered his options. Did he go get help? No... the people out here were all loonies. What could *they* do? But there was the pay phone. Yes! The pay phone outside Jade's shack. He could call his dad for help. He could... All of a sudden there was a push from behind, and he fell headfirst into the trap.

He had enough wits about him to cover his head as he fell and attempt a roll, which quite possibly saved his neck from breaking. Looking up in bewilderment, he saw the dark figures of the woman and the child above set against the smoldering desert sun. The child was standing next to the woman now, and it all made horrific sense. "And you're *next!*" the woman cackled.

Shaking his head, Jason shouted, "Oh, you fucking b—" Then a scurrying sound resonated from the dark tunnel Eddie had been dragged into. It was becoming louder and did not sound especially *welcoming*. A moan emitted from the darkness... a moan that did not belong to Eddie.

As he began to weigh his options, a voice spoke from behind him. It was the voice of a female, soft and strong. Looking over his shoulder toward the stairwell, he saw a girl who looked to be about his age. She was crouching on the last step, one hand placed against the concrete wall and the other beckoning him to join her.

"If you want to live, you gotta come with me."

Without much thought, he swiped the whiskey flask and lighter from the floor and ran to her, desperately hoping this wasn't another trap.

# 8

## Dragged Into Hell

Eddie could still see Jason through the opening of the tunnel as he was pulled backward, kicking and screaming, by malicious hands. Jason stood up, looked behind him, and fled. What did he see? Where had he gone? He had to get back to him. Some way, somehow, he was going to wrestle himself out of this and join his friend. Filled with rage, Eddie roared and placed his feet firmly on the ground, propelling his full body weight behind him. A few of the hands grappling him lost their grip, and he took this opportunity to jab his elbow behind him, landing it square in the stomach of one of the men. He heard a wail, and the two hands still clutching him fell off. Wasting no time, he sprinted toward the tunnel opening, screaming Jason's name. All the while he could hear the frenzy of footfalls behind him mixed with vicious snarls.

The opening was only a few feet away now, and as he sprinted on, his lungs felt as though they would just about burst. Then, searing pain erupted on his backside and he fell forward, his knees smashing against the hard concrete. Wincing in pain, Eddie rolled onto his back and reached for one of his knees. They were both throbbing, yet the pain in his back was screaming now. Flickering his eyes, he saw two men bend down to grab him again. Their long, stringy black hair brushing against his skin felt like sandpaper. One of them punched him hard in the stomach, and as he curled into the pain, they lifted him up and dragged him back into the tunnel again.

As he was lugged along, the tunnel opening becoming smaller and smaller, Eddie mulled over his options. Though he still put up a fight as they relentlessly pulled him through the dark tunnel, the injuries he'd sustained left him vulnerable to this pack of fiends. Was this the infamous cult that old lady had mentioned at the motel? They were actually *real?* It was fucked up. This whole thing was a bad dream... it had to be. He blinked his eyes several times, hoping to wake up in the motel room... anywhere but here. Maybe they'd just dozed off. But no, this was real. And he had to figure out how he was going to outsmart these motherfuckers. They seemed to be mere animals.

When they had reached the end of the tunnel, he was yanked to the right and dragged up a stairwell through an arched opening. The light was dim, so he could barely make out his surroundings, but he did notice the stairwell was expansive in size and curved as it ascended. Whenever he fell behind in step, he was hauled upward by the mass of freaks. As the stairs came to an end, he glimpsed to his right and saw a large room with some kind of circular device in the middle, protruding from the ground. *What the fuck?* Before he could even begin to discern what it was, his body was jerked to the left, up another curved stairwell. All that could be heard was their footsteps and the mumble of the men dragging him through this bizarre concrete structure. He didn't recognize anything they said. It was garbled, mostly grunts.

As they approached a second landing, he glanced to his right and observed a large room, in the middle of which sat a long, rectangular table. On the far side of the room there was a strange... *gateway*, of some kind. It glowed dark crimson in color. At this point, they stopped, and the men began to mumble again. How they could even understand each other was beyond him. Eddie took this opportunity to wrestle himself from their grasp, and was able to elbow one of them in the face. Prying one arm away, he turned his body with all his might from the mass of clawing hands, looking down the stairwell they had just ascended. But there was a punch to the back of his head and he bent forward, crying out in pain. Reaching forward to rub his throbbing head, his arm was quickly snagged back. The men then began to jostle him up yet another stairwell.

Before they entered the curved arched opening, however, he saw a pair of thick, spiraled horns begin to pierce through the portal, which seemed to have a gel-like consistency. He held his gaze as they tugged him upward, and just as he disappeared into the darkness of the stairwell, a massive beast emerged from the portal and stared directly at him with soulless pits for eyes. *What the absolute fuck?!* Things weren't what they seemed. This wasn't just a concrete lair of mere mortals. Whatever that thing was, it was *damn* sure not of this world.

Wretched screams could be heard as they reached what appeared to be the last landing, and Eddie was led into what resembled a torture room. On the wall facing him, a couple of men were forcing a man's wrists into a pair of thick steel cuffs that were somehow attached to the wall behind him. Glancing to the right, he noticed several chains hanging from the ceiling with sharp hooks attached to the ends. Some hooks had pieces of torn meat dangling from them. Beyond the chains sat a stone table with various nefarious tools strewn across the surface. Their sinister shapes illuminated from the dim light of candles placed on the floor throughout the room. Looking back toward the man, he noticed he had now been cuffed and was shaking his head violently, spit flying out as he desperately plead for release. Even though the man's face was contorting with utter torment, it was somehow familiar. Where had he seen that man before?

"You don't... you don't have to *do* this!! Let me go. I won't... I won't tell *anyone!* No one will know!!"

One of the fiends stood directly in front of the cuffed man and grabbed the man's chin with his left hand. Eddie was now being led to that same wall, and his heart was pounding in his chest. Fear raced through every fiber in his being, and his eyes were wide open, darting every which way. His chest heaved with each frantic breath, and it felt as though his body would explode from the adrenaline pumping through his veins. Though he fought the men dragging him to another set of cuffs against the wall, there were just too many of them.

A sharp gleam burst from behind the man's back who was still taunting the cuffed man. It was a knife, but not any knife. It was Eddie's hunting knife. *God-damn motherfuckers!* Of course, now it all made sense. He'd tried to find it after the fall, but one of them must have snagged it up first... slashed his back with it, too. He reached out an arm to grab the knife, but it was immediately snagged back. The cuffed man was still pleading for his release, and Eddie noticed the fiend release his grip from the man and mumble something as he brandished the knife in front of him.

"No!!! Don't... *Please,* don't do this!! I have a family... a mom, a dad, a sister. You can't *do* this! Don't... *Fuck!!* I can't go out this way!"

The long-haired fiend raised the knife above his head now, clenching the handle in both hands, and mumbled something indistinct under his breath. As he did so, the cuffed man's eyes widened and it appeared they would just about burst out of his face. His mouth was slack, quivering at the absolute horror unfolding before him. Then in one fell swoop, the absolute barbarian of a man lunged forward and stabbed the man directly in the forehead, the blade sinking in to the handle. A stream of blood flowed from the stab wound and the cuffed man's eyes flickered as they slowly looked up. Then there was a wet, tearing sound as the knife was pulled from his head and then plunged into the man's heart.

In utter shock, Eddie hadn't noticed he was just about to be cuffed to the wall himself. A soon as this registered, he pried an arm free and slugged one of the men in the face. Then something blunt smashed against his head and everything went black.

# 9

## Eddie

Eddie awoke to excruciating pain. There was a viscid sound... it was slithery, and had a slow and steady cadence. He turned to his right, where the sound was coming from—two men with long, ragged black hair were pulling the entrails from the man hanging next to him. As they did so, they dug into his other internal organs, feasting on them. Vomit pushed its way up his throat and he spewed whatever was left in his stomach onto himself. Metallic acid lingered in his mouth, and he yearned for water—dehydration was setting in. Looking to the floor, feeling his warm purge drip from his lips, he realized he was suspended now as well and his toes barely touched the cold concrete floor. The searing pain in his wrists greeted him for the first time, and he cringed as it burned and throbbed. Peering up, he saw thick steel bondage handcuffs clamped around his bloody wrists; the short chain connecting them hung on a thick hook embedded into the wall.

He lifted his weary gaze to the two men once again and noticed they both had upside-down crosses smeared on their faces. The cross markings shimmered in the faint light and were dark crimson in color. *What the... cannibals? Satanic cannibals?!* He knew the dead man beside him, who he'd last seen begging for his life, was not Jason. Where *was* Jason? He had to be in here somewhere—he'd fallen in, too.

Eddie played the events that had happened earlier today over in his mind with fervor. Though foggy at first, they slowly materialized. Fred at the diner, Jason's car breaking down, Jade at her shack, the lady with her child... Wait, *Jade*. She kissed him on his forehead and told him—what did she tell him? Yes, that he had so much potential... to feed some cannibalistic *psychos?!* She hammered the last nail in and was part of this whole sick plan. The lady at the motel had warned them, but how could they have known they were pawns this whole time? And Christ, that this cult was even *real*. He had to figure a way out of here... There's *always* a way.

The lifeless man's body swayed with every pull of his entrails, and Eddie fought the urge to vomit again. The men took no notice of the fact he was stirring, and the ache in the side of his head now pulsated. Then he smelled it... the stench of the room burst alive in his nostrils. Thick and rancid, it reeked of death and decay. Sweet metallic lingered in the recesses, and his mouth curled in disgust. Scanning the room, he noticed it was dimly lit by several candles placed on the floor throughout. Shadows flickered across the stone walls and flooring, and on the wall to the far right, there was a large metal table topped with glistening organs and severed limbs.

While trying to collect his thoughts, he looked in front of him and saw a girl sitting on the floor with her back slumped against the wall. Both of her legs had been jaggedly sawed off above the knee, and thick bone was visible in the stumps of raw flesh. Though a large pool of blood stained the floor beneath her, it seemed her severed limbs had been cauterized. Just raw meat waiting to be consumed now like the rest of them. Was she still alive? He fucking hoped not. Pursing his lips, Eddie began to consider his options. He couldn't go out this way. Somehow, he had to get the attention of the two men. Maybe they had the key to his cuffs. Where was the goddamn *key?!* Desperation set in as he tried to spot a small glint of metal somewhere in the room—anywhere. But there was nothing.

Eddie began to speak, but a mere moan escaped at first. Then, clearing his throat, he found the words to utter under his breath. "Let me out of here, you fuckers... I ain't gonna be your next meal." They didn't respond. The entrails of the man next to him were now completely removed and coiled up on the cold floor, a long string of purplish-blue tissue. He closed his eyes briefly in disgust and sighed out. Then a thick sawing sound reverberated within the otherwise heavy silence of the room, and he realized they were cutting through the man's sternum with a knife. *His* knife.

He spoke again, this time louder than before. "I *said*... Let me *out* of here! I swear, I'll fucking kill you both!" He swung his right leg to try and swipe one of them, but the man stepped aside. Both men were naked save for a dirty cloth wrapped around their waists. They were thin with deathly pale skin, but not malnourished—firm muscles ran along their bodies. He wondered how long they'd gone without seeing daylight. If he could, he'd swipe back his hunting knife from one of 'em and castrate them right here and now, feed them their own dicks.

They finally took an interest in him, and the one closest to him picked up the entrails slopped on the floor. He took a big bite out of the organ, then grabbed the meat from his mouth and attempted to force it into Eddie's mouth. Shaking his head left and right, Eddie tried with all his might to keep his mouth closed, but eventually the meat was forced in. He gagged instantly. The taste of the fibrous tissue was utterly repulsive in his mouth—this, mixed with the rank taste of the man's fingers, caused him to vomit once more. He gasped for air between retches, his chest heaving. The two men laughed and pointed at him, then began to eat more of the entrails themselves.

The thought of impending death was beginning to set in at this point. His only chance of survival was beating them to a bloody pulp if they ever took those handcuffs off, but he could feel the energy in his body depleting. Eddie thought of never seeing his parents again, never petting their beloved German shepherd, Ranger, again. Shit... never getting *laid* again.

At that last thought, he subconsciously looked at the woman slumped against the wall. She appeared familiar as well. Her head was now leaned back against the wall, sallow eyes beckoning for a swift death. *Shit... she's still alive.* All color had left her face, but he could tell she was once beautiful and vibrant. She must have noticed his gaze, because ever so slowly she lowered her head to look back at him. Horror shook Eddie to his core as he noticed it was her—the girl from town who had tipped them off to the mechanic. Now, here she was, with stumps for legs, dying right in front of him. He turned his gaze toward the corpse hanging next to him, and remembered she had a boyfriend with her.

A loud buzzer sounded off from somewhere in the void, and the two men abruptly slumped over toward the girl against the opposite wall. She mustered enough strength to shake her head and mouth the word "No," but her fate was sealed. They bent down, each grabbing one of her arms, and began dragging her toward an arched opening at the corner of the room. It looked as if she tried to scream, but only hoarse moans came out. She glanced at Eddie one more time as her bare flesh scuffed against the concrete, glistening tears now visible on her cheeks—and in that instant, he could tell she recognized him. He nodded to her, bidding a mournful farewell. In the silence that followed, all he could hear was his own exasperated breathing.

Moments later, the very walls began to tremble and the faint sound of buzzing machinery permeated the air... Saws.

# 10

## An Escape Plan

Carrie sat with her back against the wall in the narrow passage of bones, securing the static line she had packed with her to the jagged wooden handle of a dagger she'd found on her way down to Jason. The metal blade had gleamed from the floor of the infamous saw room in the erratic beam sent off from her flashlight. She suspected there were several weapons lurking about in this concrete dungeon. Some may have quite possibly been scavenged from the victims whose lives were ultimately snuffed out. She wasn't going down like that, though. No way. Hell or high water, she was getting out of here.

The static line turned this dagger, already wicked itself with serrated edges, into a badass weapon—she'd be able to get some good reach with it, and just hoped the knots wouldn't come loose with the force of her swings. Jason sat opposite her, staring into oblivion as her hands slowly looped around and tugged the handle of the makeshift weapon. He'd hardly said a word since he had squeezed his way in through one of the arches and joined her. Lucky for him, he just fit. Another few pounds and he would have been a goner.

When she wasn't thinking of an escape plan, she was thinking of her family. And once again, images of them arose in her mind. Her mother, father, and brothers must have been so worried by now, and there would no doubt be missing signs hung up all over for Carrie Sanchez. She hadn't told anyone about driving out here, not even them. In hindsight, it had been a terrible mistake; but she wanted to be the first of her friends to dare this notorious location.

"H-how long have you been here?" Jason whispered.

She stopped looping the rope and considered his question. The thought had never even dawned on her. "I don't know... a couple days?"

He looked to the floor before speaking again. "Well, you're doing *something* right then. *Jesus...*" Looking up to the low ceiling, "Can't imagine where I'd be if you hadn't found me. Can't imagine where... where *Eddie* is right now." He went quiet again, and she could sense the sharp fear emanating from him. "Who the fuck *are* these people?"

*"That's* the question of the hour, my friend."

"What do you mean?"

"They're not all *human!*" she whispered loudly, then held back. They had to be careful not to reveal themselves.

He shook his head at her in disbelief and squinted his eyes. "Not... *human?* Those guys I saw drag my friend away, they were human. Like a pack of wild *animals*, but still... human."

She took a deep breath in, gently placed the dagger on the ground by her right hip, and leaned her head back against the wall. "*Those* guys, yeah. But what's up *there?*" She pointed to the low ceiling above them and shook her head. "That ain't human. I don't know *what* the hell it is."

Carrie was a survivor. Just three years ago, senior year of college, her martial arts classes came to an end when she was involved in a car accident that nearly took her life. Fucker came out of nowhere, speeding through a red light and ramming into the driver's side of her white Toyota Supra. She loved that car, dammit. In the months that followed the accident, physical therapy for her broken arm and fractured ankle had lit a fire within her—the need to push through pain to excel and improve became an underlying necessity in her life. Uncanny how some events in life can flip a switch inside you, almost as if you're reborn and a new version is formed. In her case, it was Carrie version 4.0. She went through a lot of change in her youth, testing out different personalities. Though she'd settled on sweet with a bit of a bite, after the accident most of the sweetness had gone out the window.

As a result of this awakening, she'd taken a keen interest in strength training once her physical therapy was complete. She never wanted to feel that weak again. Hell, she could take Jason down no problem. But he wasn't her enemy. She'd become accustomed to being rough around the edges since the accident—it spared her pointless conversation and kept the assholes away. This conversation right now was far from pointless, though. In fact, their very *lives* depended on it. And her keen intuition confirmed Jason was a good person; he wasn't going to sabotage her. She imagined out in the real world he was easy to make friends with. Even in his current state, his voice was distinctly gentle.

Jason stared at her blankly, pondering her words. "We need to save my friend. I don't care who—or what—we have to kill. Eddie's not going to die... especially not at the hands of these sick *fucks*." He pursed his lips, then continued. "So, what's the plan? You've been down here long enough. You got one?"

*"Plan?"* She laughed softly. "I don't *have* a plan. But that lighter you got? And that whiskey? That's a damn good start." She paused, then continued. "The hole we fell through... Even if they cover it back up,

it won't be hard to break through and get outta here. Just covered by brush and dirt." She shook her head. "I was so stupid. This town… it's infamous. They like to call it the Bermuda Triangle of the desert. Once you're in, slim chance you're getting out. On a dare… a stupid *dare*, I came here. Thought I'd try my luck. See what all the talk's about, and come back with some kind of cool story. But then…" she lifted both her hands up in fists and opened them, mimicking an explosion, "*Bam!* Here I am." Squinting her large, dark brown eyes at him, she asked, "Did the kid trick you, too? Is that how you got down here?"

He shook his head and stared at the floor, not wanting to answer her question yet. "An old lady at the motel we stayed at… she warned us of some cult here. But…" He looked at her now, incredulous. "It just sounded kinda *ridiculous*, you know? Then a guy from the diner in town. He mentioned something about this area being a Bermuda Triangle, too. I thought it was just some urban legend talk or something. Turns out he was telling the truth. *Jesus Christ*, man." He looked down before meeting her gaze again, and squinted. "How are we *both* getting out of here? That drop's pretty steep, not like we can just crawl out."

She lifted the strand of static line in her hand. "You boost me up, then I'll throw this down for you and your friend. Just... obviously don't grip the blade." She had been expecting his questionable gaze, and rolled her eyes. "I'm strong—I can lift you."

He breathed in deeply, resigning to the plan, then decided to answer her question. "We weren't tricked by a kid. I mean, there *was* a kid. But it was a woman who called out to us. She had a little boy... was screaming for help. I can't believe... Like, what the *fuck?!* How is this even *happening* right now?"

"Same thing happened to me, but the opposite. Kid first, then the mom. Or, *whoever* the hell she is. Might not even be related. All I know is that we *have* to get outta here. I know you want to save your friend, so... we do that, then we bolt."

Jason's shoulders slumped. "That's just it, though. I don't even know where Eddie *is*. I don't even know how big this place is. There's different levels. He could be above us or below. *Anywhere*." Then he took a deep breath and exhaled slowly, his shoulders rising and falling as he did so. "What if we don't make it out of here? I mean, who are we kidding? We're in the nest of this, fucking... cult. I mean, he could be *dead* by now for all we know." He paused briefly, biting his lower lip, then continued. "This town. This whole town is in on it. I swear to God, we're little pawns in their *sick* game. They sent us here—to this exact location. Nearly every person we met... It was calculated."

Carrie shook her head. "It was. They're a fucking death cult or some shit." Then she leaned forward and placed her hand on his arm. "But don't think that way—don't think we're not getting outta here. You think that way, and we're already dead." There was a glint in his eyes, and she smiled, nodding.

As silent mutual agreement set in, the walls around them began to shake and the faint sound of ripping saws could be heard. Carrie closed her eyes, knowing full well what it was. More human meat being sent down the pipeline.

Jason's eyes widened, the trepidation oozing from his pores so strong she could almost smell it. Lowering his head, he pointed at her accusingly as he spoke, "What did you *see* up there? And what the hell is that *sound?*"

She shook her head. "You don't wanna know, man. It's fucking psycho shit. Like... *torture*. Not even, though. It's *beyond* torture!" Lowering her brows, she wrinkled her nose and raised her upper lip in disgust. Then, leaning forward, she bobbed her head as she spoke to clarify the absolute horror conveyed in words. "There's some kind of machine up there making that sound. Some... I don't know exactly, but... I saw a woman put into this glass enclosure or something. These concrete slabs held her in place and..." She suddenly let out a panicked cry and covered her mouth, every muscle in her body tensing up to fight in case a malevolent arm shot through one of the arches. But save for their heavy breathing, it was quiet, so she continued. "There were saws by her feet. They ripped her to shreds!"

"*What* the..." Jason leaned away, his mouth shaping to speak, but utter shock prevented any words from coming out.

"But that's not it! There's some kind of... *monster* up there. It's huge, and... disgusting! It has these insanely sharp teeth, and it fucking ate her meat! It went through this tube to—" Covering her eyes, she began to sob quietly. "If only I could have done something, but... I mean, what could I have *done?!* I don't know what that thing's capable of, and I don't wanna find out."

Suddenly a gut-wrenching scream tore through the silence. The scream of a man. It rose above an eerie, low and steady chant, and came closer and closer until it was almost directly outside of the chamber they hid within. Jason jolted up like a spring, forgetting the low-hanging ceiling, and hit his head on the hard concrete. Eyes wide and oblivious to the pain, he gasped. "Is that... *Eddie?*"

# 11

## ADRENALINE

Screaming only hastened the flow of warm blood from his stomach, so he saved his breath, though it was becoming harder and harder to breathe. The stab wound he'd received ran deep. Eddie's sight was beginning to dim as he was dragged down a curving stairwell by the two men who had stabbed him—the same men who had gutted the man next to him upstairs. Following them were countless others, all chanting something that resonated unclear.

His life flashed before him—his first baseball game, first Huffy bike, first kiss in elementary school. Angie, the girl he let seep through his fingers. Closing his eyes, warm tears streamed down his cheeks. So, this was it... this was how he was going out. He thought of how much promise there was at the beginning of their road trip. How the hell did they *get* here? So many wrong turns made. So many red flags. It was all a bad dream that had turned into a palpable nightmare.

As the stairwell came to an end, he was led into the large room he had seen before that contained some kind of sick metal torture device. *Oh* hell *no.* Now was the time to fight back, and with every ounce of strength left in his body, he pulled his arm from the grasp of the man to his right and slugged him in the face so hard he heard a crack. The man covered his nose with his hands and bent down, moaning in pain. Eddie took this chance to kick the man on his left, who was now momentarily baffled, landing his foot square in his nuts. The man fell to a fetal position on the floor, writhing in pain. With both arms free, he turned around to face about twenty other men and realized this was a losing battle. But he would go down swinging, dammit. Bending over, he pressed his hand to his stomach, wincing at the searing pain. Effectively blocking a puny fist headed straight for his head with his left arm, he then punched that fucker so hard in his stomach he felt his fist almost reach his spine.

Grinning in victory, Eddie nodded at the others, beckoning them with his hands to challenge him next. The chanting had ceased now, and the mass of pale men all squatted before him with their fists raised in readiness and defense. He threw another punch, but was blindsided by a sweep to the right leg and fell backward, his skull banging against the hard floor. Stars burst into his vision and his head lobbed from side to side as scraggly arms grasped his bare skin and picked him up, lugging him across the floor.

A loud click echoed throughout the confines of the room as the metal device was lowered into a crevice underneath it. Then one of the men walked to a far corner and pulled a large lever embedded in the floor, activating two long chains to plummet from small holes on opposite sides of the ceiling. Soon after, two more chains were pulled by men from small holes in the same location on the concrete floor. They rattled sharply along the hard surface, and Eddie felt a rush of coldness as thick metal cuffs were clamped down onto his ankles, then to his bruised and bloodied wrists. Shaking his head, a weak chuckle escaped his lips as he came to the realization that this was it. Death by goddamn chains.

The man pulled the lever more, triggering the chains above to retract, and Eddie's arms were raised and held upright. All of the remaining men had gathered in front of him now, and one of them stood directly before him, bowing his head. As he lifted it back up, Eddie spat in his face, then erupted in laughter.

"You think you got me, motherfuckers?! You ain't got *shit!!* You kill me, and I swear to *God* I'm coming for you fuckers in the afterlife." They cocked their heads, a brief look of uncertainty on their faces. "Oh yeah, that's right. *Every*. *Last*. *One* of you." Wincing in pain, he raised his right knee to clock one of them in the nuts again. His leg was suddenly jerked back, though, as the chains attached to his ankles retracted into the floor, pulling his legs out to the sides. Sneering, Eddie spat. "Didn't *like* that, huh?! Well, that shit's useless down here! Don't need that if it's all just a bunch of—" He spotted her just then in the back of the group… the woman who had lured him and Jason to the trap. Her steel gaze penetrated him so strongly, he blinked to sustain focus. Her right arm was draped around something, and as the mass teetered slightly, he saw the young boy she had been holding standing next to her with the same steel gaze. *Jesus Christ, a bunch of inbred freaks.*

Eddie heard a scream erupt from the inky darkness of the long hallway before them. He tilted his head and squinted as his lips curled up at the ends. The voice… It was familiar. Was it? Could it be? No… *Jason?*

***

As the scream ripped from Jason's core, he looked back at Carrie and saw a fury light up in her eyes that sent thrilling chills up his spine. She slowly wrapped the static line tight around her right hand a couple times, readying her makeshift weapon. He had used their time in here to find a weapon himself, and picked up the large, heavy femur bone next to his feet. They squatted there in silence, staring at each other with fierce determination as multiple footsteps scudded their way. Knowing they stood no chance of deflecting a weapon in the confines of their space, they readied themselves to climb out. She nodded at him and he nodded back. In silent agreement, they both climbed out through the arches, their bodies aching from lack of circulation. But when adrenaline kicked in, the blood surged through each of them, readying their muscles for obliteration.

Carrie stood still with her feet placed firmly on the ground. Her left hand held the slack of static line, and with her right hand she twirled the end of it like a lasso. The dagger flickered as it spun, and she grinned in delight. "You want some of this, motherfuckers?! Come and *get* it!!"

Several pale figures lurched toward them, eerie upside-down crosses marking their faces. Long, black hair veiled much of their expressions, but the glints of wicked sneers were visible. In the distance, Jason could see the others bending down and lighting a circle of candles beneath Eddie, who was now suspended in the air as the chains attached to his limbs all began to retract ever so slowly.

*"Eddie!!* I'm comin' for ya, man!"

Eddie met his friend's gaze with weary, bloodshot eyes. "J-Jason!" His voice was weak, but determined. "Kill these bastards! Kill every last one of the—" His head jerked back as the chains were pulled even tighter now, his limbs succumbing to the pressure.

*"No!!!"*

Jason launched forward as the scream cut through his throat, raising up the heavy bone clenched in his right hand, ready to smash some skulls. Carrie followed his lead, the dagger whizzing fast now, glints of light bursting in her peripheral vision as the sharp steel completed each swift revolution. Following suit, the pale figures burst toward them, the stretch of bare concrete in the middle narrowing fast with each lunge forward. Jason let out a primal scream as he raised the bone to strike and Carrie pulled back the static line, aiming for the man's throat in front of her.

# 12

## Bloodshed

With meticulous aim, Jason wielded the bone down and struck one of the men's heads hard. The man fell backward, gripping the sides of his head and bellowing out in pain. Carrie thought fast and slammed her foot on the back of the man's neck, breaking it upon impact. She stepped back, narrowly avoiding the lash of a knife from an arm whizzing by. Gaining her composure, she stared into the lifeless eyes of the man before her and swung the static line across his neck. The steel cut through deep, and blood began to gush out of the slit in his throat. Stepping backward, she raised her foot and kicked him hard in the stomach. His body fell to the ground and convulsed as blood poured out from the large gash. She looked to her left and noticed Jason was holding his own at the moment, so she let out a scream as she began to slash the other cult members unyieldingly.

Blood splattered everywhere as the serrated dagger sliced into bare flesh. Fingers were severed and faces were maimed. Every time the serrated dagger lodged into soft flesh upon swinging it, she yanked it back hard as warm blood smattered her face. She was beginning to lose steam, though. And there were so many. She had to retreat, if only for a second. Jason noticed this and followed her lead. Between the two of them, they had already taken out six. But there were so many more. And they kept on coming, mercilessly closing in.

Instinctively, Jason stared beyond the swarming mass of bodies at Eddie. It seemed he had lost consciousness now, thank God. His body was pulled so tight in all directions that tears were visible along his armpits and groin. Carrie noticed Jason's gaze and followed it. Looking back at him, she noticed he was now staring directly at her, an expression of terror mixed with seething vengeance. This span of seconds was all they needed to catch a second wind, and again they went in full force.

Carrie elbowed a man closing in on her in the throat, and as he stepped back, she worked her hand up the static line to grab the handle of the dagger. With precision, she stabbed him in the heart multiple times. Jason swung the bone in his right hand relentlessly, cracking the skulls of two men, his face now blotted a deep red. As they fell to the ground, he pummeled their faces in, rendering them bulbous chunks of red meat. They were holding their own against these heathens: two people with nothing to lose. The more blood splattered, the higher the euphoria.

As they fought on, they heard that dizzying chant begin again among the men circling Eddie. Carrie's heart dropped, because she knew what was next—they were readying for his sacrifice, and Jason's heart was about to be broken. Jason was caught off guard momentarily by the chanting, and one of the men took this opportunity to stab him in the stomach. He stepped back, howling in pain. Carrie lunged behind the man, grasping his forehead and pulling him to her, securing his head still in her grip. She cried out in pain as he sliced her thigh, then kicked the knife from his hand. Reaching for the handle of the dagger, she rapidly stabbed his throat countless times. As the blood sprayed from his arteries, covering her in metallic wetness, she grinned as he gasped for breath. She whispered in his ear, "Go to hell," then let him go. He fell to the ground like the sick piece of meat he was.

Carrie then limped to Jason's side, making sure to keep her gaze on the men before them as she did so. They were backstepping now, seeking to join their brethren in the sacrifice. Knowing she had to tend to Jason quickly, she unzipped her black hoodie and tied it tight around his waist, putting pressure on his stab wound. Looking down at the fresh blood seeping down her thigh, she was thankful the slash wasn't too deep—he hadn't hit an artery.

As she raised her head again, loud pops erupted from behind them, followed by the sound of something heavy falling to the floor. She closed her eyes briefly, a tear running down her cheek. Looking back, she saw Eddie's severed arms dangling from the chains in the ceiling. They were too late. With the mass of men they had to fight, she wondered if they'd even had a chance to save him in the first place.

*"Eddie!!!"*

Jason fell to his knees, his anguished cry so palpable it broke every last string in Carrie's heart. He clasped the sides of his head with his hands and rocked back and forth, shaking his head in utter despair. Carrie knelt down beside him and wrapped her arms around his shoulders. She couldn't avert her gaze from the macabre scene in front of them as the cult members skulked to Eddie's severed torso and began to dig into the flesh. The struggle she had faced after her own near-death experience surged hot to the surface. And now here was this young man, his life brutally snuffed out at the hands of some *sick fucks*. They needed to be stopped. This needed to end... *Now.*

Chest heaving, she stood up tall and wiped the blood from her face with the back of her hand. The cult members had now torn Eddie's torso open and were feasting on his internal organs like a pack of wild animals. Looking down to her left, Jason was kneeling and groaning in pain. She knew they didn't have much time. Swinging the static line, she lunged forward. Two of the men turned around just as she was bringing the dagger down. The serrated steel lodged in the face of one of the men, and she tugged the rope back fiercely, leaving a jagged, gaping hole in his right cheek and revealing his jaw within. As he raised his hand to his cheek in shock, she took advantage of this distraction and stabbed him in the throat, then kicked him as hard as she could in the stomach. He tumbled back onto the men behind him.

The bellowing sound of a bullhorn erupted from behind the swarming mass, and suddenly the men began to fidget, mumbling to each other in grunts and groans. What had just happened? What did the bullhorn signal? She brushed off a momentary state of confusion and again began to dodge and slice through the remaining men with her dagger. There must have still been around ten left at this point. One of them brandished a switchblade, and pain shot through her arm as he sliced her flesh. She gritted her teeth to bear the red-hot sting. It was her right arm, dammit—her dominant one. As he went to rejoin the other cult members, she stepped backward briefly, bending her legs and leaning forward, and placing her hands on her knees. Exhaustion was kicking in, but she had to keep going. It was the only way she would see her parents and her brothers again. As her chest heaved, a slow and steady rumble erupted above them. *Oh, shit.* In their bloody battle, she had forgotten all about what menacing evil lurked over them.

The sound of lumbersome footsteps resonated from within the stairwell at the far end of the room, and the men all frantically scattered to each side. As they did so, she noticed a few women as well... and the child who had lured her here! Of *course!* The women ensured the cult thrived, and that there was always fresh meat. She limped backward toward Jason, keeping her makeshift weapon ready for attack while her focus remained on the cult members. Ever so slowly, the four hooded figures she had seen earlier stepped out from the darkness of the stairwell. Two stepped to each side, their covered heads bowed and hands clasped in front of them.

"Jason... *Jason!*" She shook him to make sure he was still alive.

He looked up at her with a dim smile. "You're fuckin' badass... You know that?"

She shot him a curt smile. "You're no slacker. We gotta get outta here, though. I know what's coming, and we can't—"

The sight of an enormous figure lumbering from the dark depths of the stairwell prevented her from saying another word, and her and Jason both froze in terror. Fresh blood dripped from its trembling, gaping maw and large, hollow eye sockets seemed to somehow fixate on them. Dim bursts of light glowed red in each socket. Arching its back and looking to the ceiling, tattered and leathery black wings shot out from behind its body on each side, spanning the length of the room. An abominable roar thundered from the depths of its core, and the walls all around them began to rumble as the concrete gave way and shards began to fall from fresh cracks in the ceiling.

# 13

## A Grim Legacy

The menacing beast stood still before them, head bent down now, revealing the mass of its long, spiraled horns. Its imposing shoulders were raised and hunched forward, and thick arms were drawn back, ready to pummel. It must have been at least ten feet tall—ten feet of pure malice. Carrie had discerned some of its ghastly features in the torture room above, but now that the creature was standing before them, the realization was alarming. It embodied sheer evil, straight from the depths of hell.

Boils festered along its entire body—some had burst open, resembling bloody pockets oozing a thick black fluid from within. Its skin seemed to writhe, as if hands were roaming the fleshy canvas in angst. The flickering light from the candles surrounding Eddie's mangled torso cast grisly shadows across its face as soulless and hollow eye sockets continued to stare on, the red bursts of light inside them fiery now. A formidable growl emitted from deep within the creature as it wriggled hideous claw-like fingers, and its sinewy tail flicked across the stone floor. Then it raised one massive webbed foot, moved it slightly forward, and stomped the ground.

The resulting tremble formed a small crack that ran the length of the floor. Jason was now standing next to Carrie, and they both hunched down and shuddered in terror. The man with the bullhorn then ran to the beast. He waved his hands in the air erratically, speaking again in grunts and groans. Then he pointed at Carrie and Jason, sporting a fleshy smile revealing only a few teeth. The monstrosity slowly moved its gaze to look down at the man, tilting its head in consideration. Then it swiped its enormous arm to the left in one fell swoop, knocking the man into the back wall and smashing his head open. His lifeless body slid down the wall, revealing fresh brain matter.

Carrie's words came out in a whimper as she held her gaze on the beast ahead. "J-Jason... You still have that flask and lighter, r-right?"

"Y-yeah," he faltered, holding the same steady gaze. "In... in my back pocket. We're gonna need 'em now."

"Yes we are."

Ever so slowly, Jason reached into his back pocket, his hand finding the objects and giving them to Carrie. "Here, you do it. I..." He winced again, squeezing his eyes shut and placing his hand to his stomach as crippling pain seared through his core. "I won't do it right."

Carrie gently wrapped the static line snug around her waist, then took the objects from his hand; as she did so, the creature hunched over and a deafening roar surged from its gaping mouth. In unison, the cult members sprinted toward them in a sea of frenzied pale flesh, the beast lumbering behind. Jason and Carrie looked at each other, and as she unscrewed the lid of the flask, she screamed, *"Run!"*

He hesitated, his wide eyes a mixture of horror and concern. She nudged him with her arm. "I'll meet you down there... Go! *Now!"* As Jason limped toward the stairwell behind them, Carrie began to empty the remaining contents of whiskey on the floor, walking backward as she did so. Waiting for the members to get close enough, she then shook the flask in their direction, spattering them with alcohol. Dropping the flask, she flicked on the lighter. With her head lowered, she stared them on with furrowed brows. Letting the lighter drop to the floor, flames erupted immediately, a line of fire snaking toward the mass of snarling mouths and furling arms.

"Burn in hell, motherfuckers!!!"

Turning on her step, she bolted toward the stairwell, grabbing her backpack she had left on the floor behind them. "Jason! *Jason!*"

His voice boomed from down below. "I'm here! I'm... I made it!" Reaching the bottom of the stairwell, she hugged him fiercely, tears of relief streaming down her cheeks. When she let go and looked up at him, a boyish smile lit up his face, magnifying his adorable features. It was the first time she could really see him clearly, and kind brown eyes stared back at her from a heart-shaped face. A few strands of tousled black hair brushed his forehead. Her heart skipped a beat before reality hit again. They were almost out of this hellhole. No, they weren't home free yet, but they were so close! Screams erupted from above as the men were consumed in flames. Jason held his hands together in a stirrup. "Here, I got you. You can make it." Carrie nodded at him, stepped into his foothold, and looked up at a beautiful indigo sky. He moaned in pain as he lifted her, and her fingers scrambled to grip onto something.

She shrieked as her fingers clawed at the flat earth while the gashes in her thigh and arm screamed.

"You got this, just... There's gotta be something! Keep looking!"

Finally, she touched something cold and hard. A rock… and it had a large groove in the back she could grab onto.

"Found something!" Gritting her teeth and flexing her right leg, the tip of her shoe pressed hard into Jason's hands as she pulled her body weight up. Placing the soles of her feet onto the concrete walls for traction, she slowly inched her way above. The smooth stone offered little help, but after considerable effort she had pulled herself out and onto safe ground. Tears flooded her vision as she laughed in exalted joy. Then, wiping them from her eyes with her forearm, she quickly unwrapped the static line from around her waist and threw it down to Jason, wedging herself behind the rock for support. "Jason! Grab on!" There was silence. *"Jason!"* Scrambling forward, she looked down into the trap and saw him staring up at her with defeat in his eyes.

"Carrie… there's no hospital for hours. I'm… I'm not gonna make it. I…" He shook his head, looking down. "Hell, I don't even know where my *car* is."

"My car's not far. You can make it! Grab on!"

Jason's shoulders heaved as he looked to the ground. Then he looked up at Carrie, tears streaming down his face. "Okay, okay…" With his left hand, he looped the static line around his right hand, then held the slack of the line tight. "Okay, I… I got it."

*"Good!* Hold on tight!" There was the sound of footsteps rushing down the stairwell as Carrie wedged herself behind the rock and pulled with all her might. Jason winced as the searing pain tore through his stomach again, and he let go. "Jason, don't give up!"

Another roar erupted from deep within the bowels of the concrete dungeon. This was followed by a loud boom. Carrie scurried over the rock, staring down at Jason, who was looking toward the stairwell. He knew right away what it was, and looked up at her with a smile.

"Live a good life, Carrie. You're one helluva fighter."

Seconds later, a gully of flames burst into the trap and Jason was consumed by fire. He smiled briefly as his mom stood clear as day in front of him. She reached her arms out to him, her cherub face beckoning him to join her, and he took her hands in his.

*"No!!!"*

Carrie's guttural scream tore from deep within, and she covered her face with her arms and fell back, managing to scramble to her feet and run from the trap. Her chest heaved as she wept for Jason, for Eddie... for all the poor souls who had experienced such horrific deaths in that cold, dank, hellish tomb. She wondered how many had been taken, but the thought was almost paralyzing. Eventually, her body gave in and she fell to the earth. Placing her hands on her ears to muffle Jason's gut-wrenching screams, she sobbed into the dry desert soil. She could have saved him. If the fire hadn't erupted, she could have saved him.

Silence began to fall as Jason's harrowing screams dimmed and then were no more. Her ragged breathing was all that could be heard. A warm desert breeze swept across her skin, and the high-pitched buzz of insects in chorus was now audible in the air. Carrie's skin burned from the heat of the blast, and gritty dirt had chafed the gashes in her thigh and arm... but she was alive.

Pushing against the soil, she teetered to her knees and slowly stood up, looking to the sky. Indigo had turned to a lavender dawn, and the sun would be rising soon. She walked toward the trap, gazing down at the charred remains of Jason, and knelt down to pay her respects. "I will light a candle for you, you... beautiful soul." Warm tears fell from her eyes into his place of rest. "Thank you for saving me. I wish... I wish I could have saved you, too."

The horror of it all rushed through her being in a bloody fury, and she began to sob into her hands. She had discovered the dark secret that lurked in the grimy seams of this town, and had lived to tell the tale. As the sobs subsided and she began to catch her breath again, Carrie grabbed her backpack and stood up tall, looking toward the desert horizon. Though she had escaped literal hell on earth, she questioned whether the beast was truly gone. Despite the explosion and the cracks in the concrete, the building still stood. One thing was for sure: She'd never set foot here again.

As she limped toward the direction of the road, a deep and gravely groan could be heard from within the confines of the structure. Stopping in her tracks, she leered behind her as a soft breeze caressed her skin again. Standing still, she waited. But there was nothing.

It must have been a trick of the desert breeze.

# Afterword

I grew up in the '80s, when horror movies abounded and Freddy, Jason, and Pinhead haunted our dreams. *Death Cult* is an homage to the horror movies of my childhood—I wanted to permeate these chapters with a looming sense of dread and deliver that raw, visceral horror.

I was eight years old when I watched my first horror movie, *A Nightmare on Elm Street*. I watched it with my older brother (the oldest of two), and after hiding behind the recliner in our family room during another scary scene, he told me it was okay to watch again because nothing bad was happening. So, I did—and I was horrified! On the screen, Johnny Depp was being sucked into his bed and a hideous torrent of blood began gushing to the ceiling. I quickly hid behind the recliner again, my heart racing with what I had just witnessed. It haunted me for weeks to come, as did the entire premise of the movie. But it also sparked a dark curiosity in me.

This curiosity led me to pursue horror movies more in order to experience that same rush of adrenaline, which eventually led to scary books as well. My venture into scary books began with the beloved series, *Scary Stories to Tell in the Dark*, by Alvin Schwartz. I read those books multiple times, and the stories were so deliciously haunting. After this, I ventured to the works of Edgar Allan Poe and Stephen King. Once I experienced how fear and dread could feel so palpable in words, I began to devour their works and become inspired by them.

The idea for *Death Cult* came to me over a decade ago. I've always wanted to write an '80s-era horror book, and had written a vague outline in the early 2000s that I'd stuffed into a drawer, thinking it would never come to fruition. Over the years, the story had always beckoned to be finished, but I fought the urge to revisit it, thinking there was just never enough time in the day. I was living in New York City at the time with my husband, and the prospect of becoming an author seemed a faraway dream. But as the years went by, the story never loosened its grasp.

It was not until I published my first novella, titled *Ghost Room*, that I finally revisited *Death Cult*. As soon as I read the outline with fresh eyes again, a spark ignited within me, and I just knew these characters had to be brought to life. The story was also too fun, too vile, and too exhilarating not to be told!

It was a fun challenge to write Jason and Eddie because they are male, and I definitely found that having brothers helped me write their mannerisms and dialogue. My male beta readers were also very helpful in identifying certain conversations and scenes that just didn't flow right, and offer advice on how they could be improved to both sound and appear more realistic. It was fun writing these two characters, and I enjoyed playing their different personalities off of each other. Eddie has a carefree spirit, while Jason is more reserved, but their love of adventure brings them together on this fateful journey.

Carrie's character was not even in the outline I wrote so long ago. After revisiting this story, I knew I loved Jason and Eddie, but that wasn't enough. There needed to be another character added into the mix—and in my mind, it needed to be a female. Thus, Carrie's character was born. I feel this worked out extremely well, too, because I wanted the reader to have a glimpse into the bowels of the cult's lair before Jason and Eddie fell into the trap. Putting Carrie into that murky concrete dungeon near the beginning helped to create an underlying sense of dread in Jason and Eddie's journey.

There are hints along the way of what horrors may lurk in the ghost town they've stumbled into, but these two boys have no concept of the sheer evil awaiting them. Their journey is vastly different from hers as well, which adds a nice juxtaposition. While each step they take leads them closer and closer to formidable evil, she is already in its bowels, devising an escape plan while witnessing the horrors within.

I've always loved horror stories where the main characters are on a fateful path, and they just have a gut feeling something is awry. The departure from Jade's shack is the tipping point for Jason and Eddie. She's such a sweet thing, but what a nasty bite. The scene in her shack was fun to write, and I wanted to especially showcase Eddie's sweetness here. I chose to describe Jason in more detail at the end, while Carrie and him are devising their escape plan. And you come to know Carrie more as the story progresses.

Speaking of Carrie—I'm also a big fan of the final girl trope, and really enjoyed writing her fight for survival at the end. There's just something exhilarating about that final girl—she defies all odds with her strength, willpower, and cunning. It was great fun writing Carrie slice those cult members into obliteration, too! She was able to release all of that pent up angst from past experiences onto the evil fiends.

I feel the concept of a ghost town has mass appeal as well, and mixing up the location was a fun twist. The sprawling Nevada desert does provide a heightened sense of isolation. I grew up in Ohio and road-tripped with my family across the United States to California once as a kid. Even now, I remember driving through those desolate desert roads. Though I was safe with my family in our minivan, my imagination did run amuck as a kid. There were more than a few cars that had broken down and were left stranded on the side of the road. Thus, I chose to apply a similar outcome to Jason and Eddie's situation as well. What would it be like to become stranded out there? What possible evil could exist?

The origin of the cult is kept vague on purpose, because I wanted to leave a lot up to the imagination. I felt that by explaining it in more detail, much of the mystery would be lost. Obviously, there is a portal to hell in the concrete building and the master of the cult is the devil; but I didn't want to spell this out for my readers. Many of my favorite horror movies do not explain everything in great detail, and there's something exciting about this—our imagination can run wild with possibilities.

I want to thank my husband here as well for his enormous support. I brought this story up to him many times over the years, and he'd tell me it needed to be told; it deserved an ending. He knows how much I love horror, and delighted in reading the story as I progressed. Without his encouragement, *Death Cult* might not have come to light.

I'd like to thank all of my beta readers, too, for their invaluable feedback which helped immensely in crafting this gory tale.

We don't want our favorite characters to die, because we connect with them emotionally and are rooting for their survival. Carrie was able to make it out alive, but Eddie and Jason found themselves in a murky situation that only became more dire. And the isolation? Well, that is what drives the fear home. Maybe we can't all relate to being stranded in the desert (and hopefully not in the bowels of concrete hell), but there have been times in our lives when I am certain isolation has kicked in. Tapping into familiar and shared experiences is one of the hallmarks of horror.

I hope you enjoyed *Death Cult*, and thank you so much for choosing to read it. Out of all the horror books available, you chose mine, and for this I am extremely grateful. Please consider leaving a review or rating—these are so important for self-published authors such as myself because they help us to get noticed and continue to share our stories. Thank you!

Take care, Dear Reader... and mind those back roads.

# ALSO BY

Also by Janelle Schiecke

*Spider*

*The Clatter Man*

*Ghost Room*

## About the Author

Janelle Schiecke lives with her husband, her son, and their two cats. This is her second self-published book, and she has always reveled in horror and everything spooky.

Though she began her career editing trade magazines and nonfiction, she now enjoys delivering scares to fellow horror and paranormal fans with the stories she writes.

When she is not working on that next scary story, Janelle enjoys spending time with her family and friends, catching up on the latest streaming series and movies, and planning her next family travel adventure.

You can follow Janelle on her social media accounts below:

Twitter/X: @J_Schiecke

Instagram: @janelle.schiecke

TikTok: @janelle.schiecke

For more information, including upcoming books, feel free to visit: www.janelleschiecke.com.

Join my author newsletter for updates, exclusives, and more: substack.com/@janelleschiecke.

www.ingramcontent.com/pod-product-compliance
Lightning Source LLC
LaVergne TN
LVHW090528110826
845146LV00003B/1015